The Admirer

The Admirer

by Aurelia Osborne

Renaissance

Cover art by Caroline Frechette.
Interior design by Natasha Brousseau.

Legal deposit, Library and Archives Canada, December 2013.

ISBN 978-0-9920420-4-2

Renaissance Press
http://renaissancebookpress.com
info@renaissancebookpress.com

To my grandfather, whose name I borrowed.
I hope you wouldn't mind.
I hope you would be proud of me.

Prologue

Louisa Edwards considered herself the consummate woman of the times. She cared for the house, directed the servants, and occupied herself with the appropriate hobbies and charitable contributions. She presented herself and her house in the best possible image, and often entertained rich neighbors and influential people. If she heard the muttering of "middle-class pretensions" and "nouveaux riches" that some made around her, she simply ignored it. It was the wife's duty to further the status and the influence of her husband, and therefore her own, by any means necessary.

Her success in these endeavors helped her to forget the one great failure in her life: despite numerous attempts, over twenty years of marriage, she had failed to provide her husband with any children. She consoled herself with the utter conviction that, had God been willing to give her any children, she would have raised them to become upstanding citizens.

The proof of this bold statement lay in her ward, Rose Fraser. Rose had been the daughter of her husband's sister, and Mrs. Edwards graciously took her in when she found herself orphaned, fifteen years ago. Rose was everything Mrs. Edwards could have hoped for in a daughter: she was proper, obedient, and demure. A lifetime of work and prayer had led to this moment, the apex of any girl's education: the marriage mart. It could be their magnum opus, or their swan song. Mrs. Edwards was so determined to achieve the former, that the possibility of the latter never entered her mind. When a neighboring lady, who happened to be a peer of the realm, extended to Rose an offer of patronage for the London season, she did not see this as a gift from God, or even as a good omen: she saw it as no more than her due.

She had not expected any opposition, especially not from her husband. Mr. Edwards had allowed for the girl to have a lady's education, paying for governesses and tutors with no hesitation. But now that she was ready for her season, the end of the journey, the moment they all were waiting for, now he objected?

"The governesses came here," he explained impatiently when his wife questioned him. "I could see to both their wages and my business at the same time. London is almost 200 miles away; just the getting there will take three days at least. And to stay there for the whole summer? I won't have a business left when I return!"

As she took in a deep breath, Mrs. Edwards reminded herself that she was grateful that her husband had been present to take over the business after his father's tragic hunting accident, that she would undoubtedly find the life of a military wife exceedingly uncomfortable, and that she did not wish he had remained in the Pacific after the Crimean war. As she slowly exhaled, she plotted her arguments to convince him that his presence was necessary. It would be very awkward, and potentially dangerous, for Rose and herself to travel so far without any male protection.

"Well, you know best, my dear." Mrs. Edwards appeared resigned to her fate. "Of course, Rose and I must go. To refuse this invitation from the viscountess would be a great insult. But, since you cannot be spared from your business, I am sure we shall manage without you. I trust you have faith in my ability to act on your behalf? Someone will have to receive the offer of marriage for Rose, should any be made."

Mr. Edwards did not reply. His jaw was clenched; his complexion was turning to an unbecoming shade of red, which darkened even further as he spied his wife's slight smirk. He turned to the main object of the discussion. "Rose," he called. "What do you think of this affair?"

Rose had hoped that her guardians could settle the matter between themselves, without calling on her. She strongly disliked having to choose a side in their conflicts. Her opinion would not make any difference, and the only result would be to hurt or anger the person she sided against. Hurt her uncle or anger her aunt. Neither bode well for Rose.

She tried to be diplomatic. "I am sure that you and my aunt will do whatever is in my best interest."

Her aunt would have none of it. "The viscountess invited you to London, and offered her patronage for your London season. Do you wish to insult the viscountess by refusing her?"

"No, my aunt."

"The only way to politely refuse this invitation is to already have an agreement with a gentleman. No such gentleman came to your uncle and me to express his intentions. Have you been carrying on with someone in secret?"

"No, of course not!"

"I thought not. Since you have no serious prospects here, there is no reason for you not to go to London, is there?"

"No, my aunt."

Mr. Edwards abruptly left the room, declaring that he had arrangements to make. Mrs. Edwards, pleased to have gotten her way, instructed Rose to write to the viscountess and formally accept her invitation, informing her that they could be expected in town in a fortnight. She then rang the butler and began to make arrangements of her own.

Many frenzied days later, the Edwards and their ward left for London.

Chapter 1

The first dinner in town of the Edwards family was a simple, rich, and tense affair.

While they did send word of their arrival, they reached the house which the viscountess helped them secure, on Charles Street, at nearly five. By the time they were settled in, it was too late to call on anyone. Not that they knew anyone in town worth calling on other than the viscountess, according to Aunt Edwards.

The viscountess, though she could not call on them herself, took care of furnishing the house and providing all the necessary servants. The staff was thankfully flexible enough to include the few servants whom the Edwards brought with them, such as Eliza, Rose's maid, and Robinson, their butler, who had been with the Edwards for as long as Rose had lived with them. The usual cook, however, had been replaced by a French chef, who prepared a meal unlike any Rose had ever eaten.

Despite the deliciousness of the meal, and the wonder of finding herself in a new town, the tense atmosphere around the dinner table made Rose feel uneasy. As soon as their carriage had stopped in front of the house, Uncle Edwards had jumped out and declared that he was off to Arthur's, a nearby gentleman's club. Aunt Edwards tut-tutted him; the club was nowhere near prestigious enough to satisfy her, but she did nothing to stop him. He stayed out for two hours, only coming back at dinnertime.

Rose had hoped that the hours spent at the club this afternoon would have soothed her uncle's displeasure in coming to town, and that the satisfaction of being here would have pleased her aunt enough to lift her spirits. She had hoped for a pleasant dinner, but that hope was in vain.

Her uncle was obviously still upset. His posture was rigid, his expression somber, and he only opened his mouth to eat. Her aunt appeared to not eat at all; she was too busy making plans. They had to visit the shops, of course; Rose did not own anything fit to wear to a concert or a ball, and only possessed a few decent day dresses. Rose was expected to put on her very best dress the next day, when they were shopping. There were also calls to be paid, and it would not do for Rose to look like a pauper on her first day in town, or indeed, ever.

Rose stopped listening as her aunt expressed, once more, her displeasure at arriving in town so late in the day. Rose had heard the complaint often enough in the last few hours. Earlier in the journey, her uncle had pointed out that they would have arrived in town sooner had they taken the train. To which her aunt invariably replied that trains are noisy, dirty, and fit only for cargo, and that they were taking their carriage, as civilized people do. Perhaps Uncle Edwards made the observation once more; if he did, Rose did not hear.

Instead, she let her mind drift along the sounds of the household: the clopping of feet on the floor, the whooshing of someone rushing through a corridor, the clanging of silverware and china being gathered, the soft humming of a maid.

She thought she heard a knock at the front door, but it made no sense; the Edwards weren't expecting anyone. Perhaps it was someone knocking next door.

"That is quite enough, Rose!"

Her aunt's sharp tone brought Rose's attention back to the dining room table. She looked down and saw that she had eaten half her plate. Her aunt had very decisive opinions on the appetite of a lady, and Rose usually paid better heed to them. She put down her knife and fork.

"Leave the girl alone," her uncle replied, speaking for the first time in hours. "She'll need her strength to go through the circus you've planned for her."

"What good would it do for her to be strong if she can no longer fit into her dresses?"

"Aren't you going to the shops anyway? Let her buy bigger dresses and be done."

To say that Aunt Edwards was shocked was to put it mildly. "You... insufferable... Do I walk into your factories and tell you how they should be run? No, I do not. This is my affair, and you will kindly let me run it my own way. I know best."

The sound of a throat clearing interrupted the discussion.

"Begging your pardon, madam, sir" said Robinson.

"What it is?" asked Aunt Edwards.

"A message was just delivered for Miss Rose."

7

"Well, take it back! Whoever sent it should have better sense then to deliver messages during dinner time. Let him come back at a more decent hour."

Aunt Edwards's tone was harsh. Harsher, perhaps, than it would have been had she not been so upset with her husband. But, regardless of the tone used, the lady of the house had spoken, and all Robinson could do was leave the room, with a small bow and a quiet "Yes, madam."

The table was cleared, dessert was brought up, and Rose was left with the difficult task of calculating exactly how much of said dessert would be too much, and therefore further upset her aunt, and how much would be too little, which would in turn insult the chef.

After dinner, the family retired to the sitting room. As Uncle and Aunt Edwards each took a seat in their respective chair, Rose made her way toward the piano.

"Rose." Her aunt's call stopped Rose in her tracks. It was not as harsh as the dinner reprimand; the tone was conversational rather than chiding.

"May I not play the piano tonight, my aunt?" Rose knew the answer, even as she asked the question, but she held out hope nonetheless.

"No, you may not," replied Aunt Edwards. "I have told you before, child, you are much too proficient on the instrument as it is. No one wants a braggart for a wife. Take some needlework instead."

She would have preferred to play, especially on that night, when the mood was so dark. Rose had so much on her mind: being in town for the first time, the current state of disharmony between her aunt and uncle, the necessity to find a husband who would get her guardians' approval, the hope that her fiancé would be a man she can have a loving relationship with, the fear of making such an utter fool of herself that she would ruin her chances of happiness forever. Music would express her worries better than words could, and she had much hope that by driving her disquiet into the world and out of her mind, she would find some peace.

But it was not to happen, not at that moment. Aunt Edwards had spoken. Rose picked up the needlework she had started back in Yorkshire, and took a seat.

Her uncle read the evening newspaper. Her aunt read from a small book of poetry. Rose embroidered a handkerchief. The silence was oppressive.

It was Robinson who broke the tension once more. "I'm terribly sorry for the interruption, but there is the matter of Miss Rose's message."

"Have you not sent it back?" The news did nothing for Aunt Edwards's mood; as mistress of the house, she expected her orders to be obeyed without question.

"I intended to, madam, but I'm afraid that I returned to the door to find the messenger gone."

"Well, bring it in," said Uncle Edwards. "Oh, do not frown at me, my dear. I know you are as curious as I am to find out what this mysterious missive says, and who sent it."

Rose laid down her needlework as Robinson approached her. He handed her an intricately folded piece of paper, bearing her name.

"Well?" asked Aunt Edwards, as Rose was silently reading the note. A more observant person than Mrs.

Edwards might have noticed that Rose was struggling to control her breath and her voice, or how tightly she was holding the paper, until her joints were white and her hand was trembling.

"It only says welcome to town."

"Who sent it?"

"I do not know, my aunt. There is no signature and no seal."

"Robinson, who delivered it? What can you tell us about his appearance?"

"Nothing, madam. He was but a street urchin."

Before her aunt could express her displeasure at the butler's unsatisfying report, and at the idea that anyone would use a street urchin to deliver any kind of message, Rose asked permission to retire for the night.

"Oh, very well. Remind Eliza to prepare your sea green day dress for tomorrow. You must be especially careful with your appearance, since you have already been noticed."

Rose promised that she would, and, after wishing a good night to her aunt and uncle, she left the room while her aunt resumed her interrogation of Robinson.

***

Rose was pacing in front of the fireplace in her room, holding her anonymous note. It was no more than that, a note, much too short to deserve the name of letter or missive. It was only a few lines, but those lines chilled her to the bone.

> And so you arrive, Miss Fraser, to London town,
>
> Like a little country mouse walks into the viper's nest,
>
> Beware, you meek and feeble thing, not to be swallowed whole

Rose could not decide what to do. She told herself that she was overreacting. It was a jest, nothing more, a jest of poor taste, and she ought to throw the note in the fireplace and forget all about it.

Yet she could not bring herself to do it. A jest this may be, but people did not act without a reason, and she could not fathom an explanation for someone, anyone, sending her this note. The best she could hope for was to uncover the identity of her... she was not sure what to name the person who wrote this. "Admirer" was altogether the wrong term. "Tormentor" felt too strong, after only one note. "Correspondent" suggested that she was writing back to him, which she had neither means nor intentions of doing.

The... taunter, as she finally settled on, would not stay anonymous very long. She had seen enough little brutes playing this kind of game to know. He would want to get a better look at her reaction, enjoy the fruits of his labor, so to speak, and he would betray himself. When he did, she would be able to face him and get some sort of explanation.

He would probably deny it, of course, unless she could provide some proof. So she kept the note, put it in a drawer, and resolved to put the matter out of her mind for the night.

But as she lay in her bed, falling into an uneasy sleep, she could not shake the suspicion that something more sinister than a mere jest was afoot.

Chapter 2

The next morning, another letter awaited Rose. Thankfully, this one was signed, and of an entirely different nature.

Dear Miss Fraser

Welcome to London. What a grand time we shall have together, I am sure.

I have already informed our friends of your arrival, and I would not be surprised if you had many invitations to tea and to dinners by the end of the day. I therefore officially claim my privilege as your patroness, and request your presence to the ball I give this Thursday night. I have included an invitation. Now, Miss Fraser, you must come. I will not take no for an answer.

I have also taken the liberty to open accounts in your name at some of my favorite shops. I know young ladies prefer to be dressed in the latest fashion when they are introduced to the beau monde. I have included the list as well, and I trust Forrester will have no trouble finding them.

Until we see each other again, please accept my best wishes for your health and happiness.

Yours truly,

Lady Frederica de Courcy, Viscountess Latimer

"Well," said Mrs. Edwards after Rose shared the letter with her. "That is excellent news indeed." She took the list of shops out of Rose's hands. "I shall give this to Forrester while you write a reply to the viscountess. We leave for the shops after breakfast."

With these instructions, Mrs. Edwards left to find Forrester, the coach driver that Lady de Courcy had so graciously provided for the duration of their stay in London. Rose could not help but sigh as she made her way back to the library, or more specifically the writing desk and correspondence material lying therein. It was going to be a very long week.

And a long week it was, indeed. Every day was the same. Breakfast, then a ride to the shops. The only delay Mrs. Edwards had allowed was to go to church on Sunday. In the shops, Rose endured hours upon hours of measurements, advice on fabric samples and patterns, and false praises.

Everywhere she went, it was the same thing. "Stand up straight, now, Miss. Fraser." "What beautiful, chestnut locks you have!" "You must get rid of this ridiculous crinoline. How passé. A bustle is much more flattering." "This shade of pink plays off beautifully against your skin. Such perfect complexion." "No wardrobe is complete without a Dolly Varden dress." "I just happen to have the perfect color to match this fabric to your eyes. It would be a shame not to play off those bewitching features."

Rose assumed that it was Lady de Courcy's influence that brought such a reaction, and she almost wished that the viscountess had not given herself the trouble. It was overwhelming enough to navigate this sea of fabrics, colors, and styles, not to mention all the accessories and the all-important question: crinolette or full bustle?

Rose spent hours listening to the essential qualities of cotton, wool, satin, and silk, to name just a few, or the distinction between apple green and sea green, or peacock blue and royal blue, or the various attributes that distinguished the ball gown from the tea gown and the seaside dress, or even, in one case, a very strong and passionate debate between the virtues of the Pre-Raphaelite style and those of the Dolly Varden. After all that, she simply no longer had the energy to gracefully accept such ridiculously exaggerated raves. Chestnut locks and bewitching eyes, indeed.

The discomfort of the shopping experience was increased tenfold by the arrival of a second, unsigned note on Monday.

The pretty ribbons and colorful chiffons

Do not hide who you really are

Such an abhorrent disguise disgusts me

The country mouse transforms into a city cat

There was no doubt in her mind that the two notes had been written by the same person. The taunter must therefore be someone who knew that she spent most of her days shopping. Unfortunately, her routine had never been made secret, so this did nothing to help her discover the identity of the man in question.

She did with this note what she did with the first: put it in a drawer and out of her mind, as best she could.

After the shops, they returned to the house for a quick lunch and a review of the invitations that had arrived in the morning.

Invitations such as this one:

You are cordially invited to an afternoon tea

This Saturday, May 4th

Four o'clock

With Mrs. Harold Parker

24 Down Street

***

"I'm terribly sorry that my invitation came on such short notice," said Mrs. Parker as she greeted Rose and her aunt on Saturday afternoon. "But I'm afraid it couldn't be helped."

"It is no trouble at all, Mrs. Parker. We are grateful for the invitation."

Mrs. Parker dismissed Mrs. Edwards and turned to Rose. "I'm sure you don't remember me. We only met once, three winters past or so, when I was visiting Lady de Courcy."

Rose, as a matter of fact, did have a vague memory of Mrs. Parker and her husband. They had all been to a dinner party organized by the viscountess. She had played Für Elise after dinner, and Mr. and Mrs. Parker had complimented her. But it would probably be rude to point that out to her host now.

"It is a pleasure to meet you again, Mrs. Parker."

Mrs. Parker, satisfied with Rose's answer, turned back to Mrs. Edwards. "And how do you find London, Mrs. Edwards?"

"I find that I like it very much. So much activity and excitement is a relief after the dreariness of the North."

"'Tis your first time in the city, is it not?"

"The first in many years. But with all the changes that have occurred since, it feels as though I was discovering a new town altogether."

"Yes, is it not a wonderful time we live in? I can hardly believe all the wonders of technology that man has achieved. An underground train, who would have thought? And telegrams that can be sent all the way to America?"

"Indeed."

Mrs. Edwards took a few bites out of a chicken salad sandwich while Mrs. Parker sipped some of her tea, before speaking up again.

"Really, you could not have chosen a better time to come into town. With the season upon us, there is nothing to be had but parties and amusements. I suppose you're off to get this young lady married. Well, Miss Fraser, what are your prospects?"

The bluntness of the question shocked Rose into silence. Even as Mrs. Parker's giggle indicated that the question had been meant as a tease, her aunt's stare let her know that she took the question very seriously, and that the wrong answer would have dire consequences.

"I... I believe that my prospects are as fair as the next girl's, Mrs. Parker."

"I should hope so, for your sake!" Mrs. Parker laughed once more as she took another sip of tea. "Oh, come now, Miss Fraser, I was only teasing you. I'm sure that you have everything to make a very good match. A comely girl such as yourself, pleasant and proper, with no scandalous relations or disgraceful past. The only possible mark against you would be the assumed lack of education, with you coming from the North. You are educated, though, aren't you?"

"Yes, madam. My aunt and uncle hired tutors for me."

"Marvelous! You have been taught languages and art, then, along with the rules of etiquette?"

"I have, Mrs. Parker."

"Good, good. Did you learn French or Italian?"

"French, madam."

"All the better. I've always found Italian pretentious. Do you draw and paint as well?"

"I draw, a little. But I am afraid that my skills are very poor."

"Oh. What of music? Do you sing and dance? Do you play?"

At that moment, Rose realized something that made her feel very silly, for truly she should have noticed earlier: it was Mrs. Parker who didn't remember their first meeting. And truly, how vain of Rose to expect to be so memorable, three years after the fact.

"I do sing, and dance. I also play the pianoforte."

"The child is being modest," said Mrs. Edwards. Apparently, there was no harm in her bragging about Rose's musical abilities. "She would do nothing but play if we didn't drag her off the instrument. But her perseverance pays; I've heard nothing but compliments about her playing."

"Is that a fact? You enjoy music, Miss Fraser?"

"I do, madam."

"Have you been to a concert yet? No, probably not, if you've just arrived in town. Well, I'm sure you would enjoy them very much. And the opera, too. You must go to the opera, as soon as you possibly can. It's a wonderful experience. Mr. Parker and I are going to see La Vie Parisienne tonight. In fact... is this the time? My good Lord, I'm afraid I have to go get ready. Say, if you have no other engagement, would you like to accompany us? I'm sure we could find you some seats, there are always a few unsold tickets."

"I am afraid we are already engaged for dinner," replied Mrs. Edwards.

The three women rose from their seats.

"Oh, what a pity. Some other time, then. And Miss Fraser, you must come and dine with us someday, that I might hear you play the piano."

Rose assured that she would, then she and her aunt said their goodbyes and were escorted to their carriage.

"The woman has all the sense of a doorknob," declared Aunt Edwards once the carriage was safely on its way. "But she has connections, and connections are what we need. You did well, Rose."

"Thank you, my aunt."

"You will have a little time to rest when we get back to the house. Use it well, you will need all your wits at the dinner party tonight."

"Yes, my aunt."

And so it went, from tea to dinner and back to tea again, the parties and introductions all succeeding each other.

The number of these invitations was manageable, at first, but as the days went on, and as Rose's reputation grew around town, it became impossible to accept them all. Even by going to tea with one acquaintance, and to dinner with another, and then to the theater with yet another, which is what Rose did most days, there was simply not the time call on all who wished to be called upon.

Such a success, so early, made Mrs. Edwards the happiest of women. She liked nothing more than to decide who was the most influential, the best to be seen with, and then order Rose to reject any conflicting invitations. The simple fact that there was a conflict filled her with bliss; when there was a choice, one could choose the best, when there was no choice, one made do.

In one instance, she was forced to make do, and for that she refused to speak with her husband for three days. It was his sentimentality that cost them a precious evening.

It was on the fifth day of their stay in London, two days before the ball of Lady de Courcy. The long days and the stress of the anonymous notes were beginning to take their toll on Rose, and she wished for nothing more than a quiet evening at home, playing her piano. She tried not to linger on this fantasy too much, for it had no hope of becoming reality.

It had pleased her to find an invitation to dinner with the Jones. The two families had been neighbors in the North, and their eldest daughter, Mary, was Rose's age; the two girls had been playmates, years ago.

Aunt Edwards, on the other hand, had no such attachment to the family. "A barber, for the love of God, elected to the House of Commons," she said when the invitation arrived. "There is nothing to be gained in such low acquaintances. It is just as well that you separate yourself from that girl. From what I hear, she is turning quite wild. This is one case where you must be firm in your refusal. Let it be made clear that you will have nothing to do with this family."

"Which family?" asked Uncle Edwards as he walked into the room.

"The Jones. Can you imagine that they had the cheek to invite us to dinner?"

"I've no need to imagine it, dear. Mr. Jones delivered a similar invitation in person when I met him at the club today. I've already accepted."

"You..."

"After days of running around in town, never a moment's rest, I thought it would be nice to have a simple dinner with our friends and neighbors. The matter is quite settled, I'm afraid."

"But, Mr. Edwards," said Aunt Edwards as she struggled to keep her composure, "I do wish you had not made such hasty plans without consulting me. We already get more invitations then we can accept; if we do not take care..."

"My dear, I'm quite happy to let you take charge of this campaign, as it's of no interest to me. However, the Jones have been our friends for near twenty years. If I'm going to be spending the next few months making small talk with strangers, I want one evening with my friends."

Uncle Edwards had yet to accompany Rose and her aunt on even one outing, preferring to spend his days at the club and his evenings at the pub, but Rose kept silent. Perhaps her uncle meant that he wanted one evening with friends first, and would begin to accompany Rose and Aunt Edwards in town soon. Besides, Rose wanted to accept the dinner invitation; her uncle's intervention suited her perfectly.

Aunt Edwards seemed set to argue her point when Mr. Edwards spoke again. "As I've already said, Mrs. Edwards, the matter is settled."

And, to Rose's joy and Aunt Edwards's chagrin, so it was.

This was the most pleasant dinner Rose had experienced in a week. Her uncle was cheerful, merrily debating various issues with Mr. Jones. Her aunt was quiet, and she listened to Mrs. Jones gossip as gracefully as she could, considering her displeasure. The reversal of moods did much to improve the ambiance.

Rose was very happy to see her friend Mary, even though she had the distinct impression that something was different about her. It was not her appearance; physically Mary was as she had always been: tall and vigorous, with bold red hair and dark eyes.

It was their discussion, after dinner, that did not sit right with Rose. She had joined her friend as Mary took her seat as far away from her parents as the small sitting room would allow.

"How are you, Mary?"

"I am fine, Rose. Much better than you, I would say. Poor dear, you are being dragged to the marriage mart, after all."

Mary had very strong opinions on marriage, which she had relayed to Rose on many occasions in the past. Marriage, according to Mary, was the worst thing that could happen to a woman: being forced to produce baby after baby until you died from it. She swore never to let herself become any man's property.

"'Tis not so bad," replied Rose softly.

She wondered, as she had many times in the past, if her friend realized how fortunate she was to even be able to entertain such ideas. Though it had never been specifically stated, Rose knew well that she would only be allowed to leave her aunt's house in one of two ways: married or thrown out on the streets. In her younger years it was the fear of being sent to the orphanage that kept her well behaved. As she grew too old for the orphanage, she realized the options of a young girl with no family, no skills and no money were very few, and much worse.

"Yes, you likely believe so. Well, since I'm sure you've done nothing but tour the beau monde in the last few days, we have no choice but to talk about them. Have any of the society matrons made an impression on you?"

"I must confess that of the ten ladies who have entertained us in the past four days, none made a distinct impression."

"Good lord! That many? No wonder they all blend together. And what about their sons? Did you catch the eye of some lucky gentleman?"

That innocuous comment brought the two unsigned notes to the forefront of Rose's mind. "No," she said nonetheless. It was not the kind of attention her friend had meant, to be sure.

"You are lying." Mary's hushed tone did not mask her exaltation. "I can tell, you've always been a rotten liar. Who is it? What does he look like? Where did you meet him?"

"I didn't... That's not... I just... I have received notes. Two of them, unsigned. That is all."

Mary stared at her flustered friend, as the poor girl tried to regain her composure. "Rose Fraser," she finally said, "you have a secret admirer."

"If you could call it that," mumbled Rose.

"You great goose, why do you get so upset about this? This is the perfect relationship. You just go out and be your charming self, and you let him go through the trouble of paying you compliments. You don't even have to pretend to like him."

"I would rather go through the normal steps of courting, beginning with a proper introduction. And since when do you believe in relationships? I thought you'd sworn them off."

"I swore off marriage."

"And the first leads to the second, so what is your point?"

Mary stared at Rose as if she was missing something very obvious. Before Rose could figure it out, or ask for further explanations, Mrs. Jones invited her to entertain them on the piano. As she had not played since she left the North, Rose accepted with great pleasure. After a few songs, the game tables were pulled out. The evening ended before Rose had a chance to speak to Mary alone again.

***

Rose was thinking about her conversation with Mary as she stepped off the coach and made her way into her house. What kind of relationship did not lead to marriage?

It's possible that one of the parties might die, or that the engagement be broken off for some reason. But in both cases, the intent had clearly been to marry. A relationship where neither party intended to marry... that would mean... No, surely Mary wouldn't...

"Miss Rose."

Rose was startled to find Robinson standing in front of her. She found herself shocked to be staring in his eyes; she could never quite shake the impression that Robinson should be taller than her. He was handing her a small silver plate, and on the plate was an intricately folded piece of paper.

Another one.

Rose suppressed a sigh as she picked up the note. "Thank you, Robinson."

Robinson bowed and turned to leave when Rose called out to him. "Robinson!"

"Yes, miss?"

"You have said that these notes are delivered by a street urchin?"

"Yes, miss."

"Always the same one?"

Robinson hesitated a moment before he replied. "I'm afraid I couldn't say."

"Rose! Stop pestering Robinson and get to your room."

"Yes, my aunt. Goodnight, Robinson."

"Goodnight, miss."

In her room, with the door safely closed behind her, Rose opened the note.

Can you recognize your true friends

From the ones who would stab you in the back?

Can you do it before it is too late?

Was this about Mary? But that made no sense. The decision to dine with the Jones was made at the last minute. There was hardly any time for whoever this man was to find out about it and then write the note. And still, the coincidence would be too great to explain otherwise. Rose caught herself wondering whether Mary was the true friend, or the one who would stab her in the back.

But the thought lasted only for a moment, and then Rose resolutely pushed it away. She refused to let this stranger, too cowardly to name himself, dictate who she could and could not associate with. She had enough of that from her aunt, thank you very much. She would not let that man make her doubt her oldest, dearest friend.

Rose shoved this note in the same drawer which held the other two and slammed it shut. She gripped the edge of the bedside table and took in several deep breaths. There was no use in denying it: she was being watched.
And there was nothing she could do about it, but hope

that the man would either reveal himself, or get bored and stop.

She did not have much hope of either happening.

Chapter 3

By Thursday night, Rose had put the matter of her 'admirer' sufficiently out of her mind. With Lady De Courcy's ball approaching, there was much to do. Mrs. Edwards whipped herself into a frenzy, trying to regain the social capital lost in the "Jones affair", as she had taken to calling the dinner with their old neighbors, and she naturally dragged Rose along with her. Added to the numerous outings were dance lessons to refresh her memory, and final fittings for her ball gown. Rose hardly had the time to sleep or eat, let alone worry about things which she rationalized were out of her control anyway.

Rose crossed the threshold of the De Courcy London residence as the clock struck eight, accompanied by her aunt, and determined to have a pleasant evening.

The first thing she noticed upon entering the ballroom was the orchestra. They were playing Chopin's Grande Valse Brillante, a common enough occurrence, since the piece has been well liked for many years, but something was strange about it, a touch awkward. It took her a moment to figure out what the problem was: they were playing the piece allegro when it was clearly meant to be vivace. This was not a promising start.

Rose gritted her teeth and kept her polite smile firmly in place. It appeared that their hostess shared her aunt's opinion that arranging for proper musicians was not a necessary expense when one entertained, even if one was giving a ball, where music played such an important part of the evening. Rose respectfully, but very quietly, disagreed.

She noticed Lady Frederica De Courcy, Viscountess Latimer, second. Her Ladyship's estate was less than a mile away from Rose's hometown, and it was her habit to invite all the most important townspeople to her frequent dinner parties, including Rose's uncle and aunt. The viscountess, in fact, had taken a liking to Rose, and it was in no small part thanks to her offer of patronage that Rose could have a proper London season. She would have been quite upset had she known that she was not the first thing to grab Rose's attention. Thankfully, though her ladyship had many great qualities, clairvoyance was not among them.

"Dearest Miss Fraser," exclaimed the viscountess as she approached her new guests. "Don't you look ravishing tonight, simply ravishing! And Mrs. Edwards. How do you do?"

Rose and her aunt offered the usual salutations with a small curtsy.

"Well, Miss Fraser, what do you think of my little soiree?" The viscountess referred to any gathering of her friends and acquaintances as 'little soirees', whether it was a dinner party at her estate in Yorkshire or a London ball.

"I can hardly believe my eyes, Your Ladyship," answered Rose. Or her ears, though she knew better than to say that bit aloud.

"Well, come in, come in. I cannot have you standing in the doorway, it is simply ridiculous. It will not do. I will not be satisfied until a young gentleman stands up with you on the dance floor. Now, who is here?"

A great many people were there, and a fair number of young gentlemen among them, but it appeared as though none would satisfy her Ladyship's sensitivities. The man was either lacking in character - "A positive rake!" her Ladyship would announce. "I would not even invite him if his dearest mother wasn't such a good friend of mine. I can't bear to insult a friend." - or lacking in situation - "He is such a dear man" her Ladyship explained, "but he hardly has 100 pounds in his own name. Surely you can do better." - and the young man would be immediately rejected. Sometimes it was Rose who was lacking in situation - "My dearest Miss Fraser, if it was up to me, I would see you engaged to the Prince of Wales himself, this very night. But, alas! 'Tis not the way of the world." - but fortunately, never in character. Rose and Aunt Edwards followed the viscountess in silence, both acknowledging that they had little expertise to bring to the situation.

"Aha!" her ladyship exclaimed, having finally settled on a potential suitor for Rose. "There he is. I knew I had seen him earlier."

"May I ask to whom Your Ladyship is referring?" asked Aunt Edwards.

"Why, to the young Mister Grey, the youngest son of the Baron of Rotherfield, of course."

"The youngest son, milady?" Mrs. Edwards insisted.

"Yes, youngest of three sons. He has no hope of getting the title, of course, especially since the eldest son is already married with a child on the way. But still, he is a peer of the realm, and he has a very decent inheritance due. Not to mention his profession, unusual though it may be, which pays very well, from what I gather. I shall fetch him and introduce you."

The viscountess kept her promise, leaving Rose and her aunt standing in their spot, with plenty of speculations and unanswered questions about the nature of Mister Grey's unusual profession.

***

James Grey took pride in being a rational man, one who did not make assumptions or form opinions until he had all the facts. So it was with the greatest confidence in his own judgment that he labeled his friend Robert Cowper the worst schemer in all of England. His plots never worked, and they usually spelled trouble either for Cowper himself, or for the friends he dragged in with him.

Cowper's plot was that much less likely to succeed, that it was fueled by his admiration for Lady Newport, the most desirable debutante on the market.

"I won't be a part of this."

"But you have not even let me explain..."

"I have no need to. I have enough firsthand experience to know that the words 'I have a plan', coming out of your mouth, are a recipe for disaster."

"Not this time, old chap. I'll admit that, in the past, some miscalculations on my part have let us both to near disasters. But this is different," insisted the young lover to his skeptical friend. "I have been using your technique."

This intrigued James enough to make him pause for a moment. "Have you now?"

"I have. I spent quite some time studying the lady and preparing my approach. I have noted, among many other significant details, that she is most often seen in the company of Lady Dunwich, whom you can see here dancing with Thornton."

James noted Thornton's partner, a pleasant enough looking girl, though she was nothing to Lady Newport. The ladies had the same fair coloring, but whereas Lady Newport's was natural, her friend's was artificial. The treatment had brought damage to Lady Dunwich's hair, as it usually does, and she was now forced to either hide it under a bonnet or, as was the case at the moment, distract from it with a wreath.

"They go to every assembly, every ball, and every concert together," continued Robert. "They even share a chaperon. They are first cousins, you see, and as close as sisters from what anyone can tell. Observe. The dance is ending, both ladies are taken back to their chaperon. Lady Newport is immediately called upon to dance again. It'll come as no surprise to you that the lady's dance card was filled up within minutes of her arrival. Lady Dunwich, on the other hand, is forced to sit this one out. Now, look at Lady Newport. She is still smiling, but the expression is forced, her posture is more rigid than a moment ago. And there, did you see that? As she turned and faced the position where her friend remains seated, she drops the facade entirely, if only for a second. It is obvious that she finds little pleasure in her own success, when her friend is not equally blessed."

"Indeed. So what is the plan?"

"Well, I was lucky enough to secure a dance with Lady Newport, the dinner dance, if you please, and I intend to use my time on the dance floor to make the best impression possible. Which, of course, would be a much simpler task if Lady Newport was in a pleasant state of mind, a feat that I believe can only be achieved if Lady Dunwich is also on the floor. So the plan is this: as I make my way to the ladies and their chaperon, you accompany me. I introduce you, you invite Lady Dunwich to dance, she accepts, and as I do my best to dazzle Lady Newport, you do your best not to insult her friend, so that I may show my face again in their company."

James took a moment to consider as he observed his friend. Much of Cowper's plan relied on his ability to dazzle Lady Newport; a challenging but not impossible task. True, Cowper had nothing to make him stand out in a crowd; his looks, his sense of fashion, his height, everything about him was average. But he was definitely a pleasant fellow, and he had the wit and the charm to make himself appear handsomer than he was.

"I have to admit, Cowper, considering your poor history, I did not expect such a simple and relatively well thought-out plan. This might be your most successful endeavor yet."

Mr. Cowper was rather proud of his friend's praise. "You have always said that any man can apply the concepts of observation and deduction to the solving of problems, it is simply that no-one takes the time and effort."

"I'm glad to be proven right, in this particular instance at least."

"So you'll help me?"

"I didn't say that."

"Grey!"

"There is one key element that you have not taken into consideration, and which may make my implication in the affair entirely futile: Lady Dunwich may already have a partner for the dance in question."

"And if she doesn't?"

"Should both Lady Dunwich and I be available, it will be my pleasure to help you."

"What do you mean, should you be available?"

"I mean that there is one person who has to power to call me, and you, and any other fine gentleman present here, to the dance floor, at her whim, and we have no choice but to obey."

"And who is that?"

"Good evening, Mr. Grey, Mr. Cowper."

The gentlemen turned and bowed to their hostess, Lady de Courcy.

"Were you just speaking of the dear Lady Dunwich? Such a sweet girl. What a shame that she has to sit even one dance out. Mr. Cowper, I have introduced you earlier this evening, haven't I? I'm sure it would be no trouble for you to go and invite her to the next dance, unless you're otherwise engaged?"

James suppressed a smile as his friend could do nothing but bow and accept the mission given to him by the viscountess. It was the duties of the host to ensure that no lady in attendance turned into a wallflower, as discreetly as possible, of course. When called upon to escort a lady, the well-bred gentleman had no choice.

"Excellent," declared Her Ladyship. "Now, Mr. Grey, I require your company."

"At your service, milady."

***

Rose and Mrs. Edwards were not left to question themselves for very long, for almost as soon as she left, Lady de Courcy returned with a young gentleman.

"Mr. Grey, allow me to introduce to you Miss Rose Fraser, and her aunt, Mrs. George Edwards. Miss Fraser, Mrs. Edwards, I present to you the Honorable James Grey."

Rose curtsied to the young man, whom she perceived as exceptionally tall, with a wide, handsome face and a pleasant smile. James bowed down to the young lady, whom he judged to be very pretty, with delicate features and an unexpected depth in her eyes.

"Mrs. Edwards was my neighbor in the North," continued the viscountess. "The family has just arrived in town."

"And how do you like London?" asked James.

"It is a bustling city," replied Mrs. Edwards.

"I am glad to hear you say so. One tends to be prejudiced about one's hometown; it is a good thing to have our opinion confirmed. Miss Fraser, will you do me the honor of dancing with me?"

"With pleasure, sir," replied Rose.

She offered her dance card to him. He briefly considered reserving one of the more significant dances, as his friend Cowper had done with Lady Newport, but he rejected the idea almost immediately. For one thing, choosing a later dance would mean leaving and coming back, with more small talk and awkwardness. For another, James was certain that, had Cowper been given the opportunity, he would have danced the first dance with Lady Newport. James had that opportunity with Miss Fraser, and he took it, putting his name for the very next dance, which was just about to start.

Miss Fraser's smile as she took back her dance card and saw which dance he reserved gave him some confidence. It was, he hoped, a sign that he had made the right choice.

He took her by the hand and led her to the dance floor as the next dance was announced. The dancers assumed their positions. The first notes of a lively polka stirred the air, and the dance floor came alive.

The couple's first dance was very tense at first. They were both fully aware that they only had a few minutes to make the best impression on their partner, and the possibility of failure terrified them. Etiquette demanded that James be the first to speak, but he could not think of anything to say. The only thing that came to his mind was, for God's sake, man, do NOT speak of the weather. DO NOT SPEAK OF THE WEATHER.

"It was very kind of Lady de Courcy to invite you."

James wished he could kick himself at that moment. It was even worse than speaking of the weather! He sounded as though he thought that Miss Fraser somehow did not have the right to be in the ballroom.

Rose, on the other hand, rejoiced in the opportunity. She had hoped to ask Mr. Grey about the viscountess's allusion to his profession, but had not known how to bring about the subject.

"Yes," she replied. "I'm very grateful for her generosity. Have you known her long?"

"All my life, it seems. She was a friend of my late mother, and a great source of comfort for the whole family when she passed away."

"That is... very nice, and touching."

Rose could not think of a way to reply to this new information. She felt terrible, bringing up the subject of Mr. Grey's profession now, after such an unexpectedly moving declaration, but her curiosity was greater than her self-disgust.

"The viscountess mentioned that you have an unusual profession."

"Did she? I'm surprised you brought it up."

"You're right. It was incredibly forward of me, inappropriate. I apologize."

"No, not at all, I assure you. I find it charming."

James could see that his reassurance did not reassure Miss Fraser. He spoke the truth, though. He was charmed, intrigued, and even relieved, to be honest. He felt very confident in his skills and expertise, and he felt much more at ease discussing this than many more socially acceptable subjects. His admiration grew for the young lady who was brave enough to broach such a subject upon their first acquaintance.

"I am a private investigator," he continued.

Rose pondered over the expression for a moment, as she had never heard it before.

"I'm afraid I do not know what that means."

Mrs. Parker's words rang in Rose's ears: "Mark against you... lack of education, with you coming from the North". Would Mr. Grey take her for an ignorant country girl? Would every word out of her mouth continue to damage what little esteem he might hold for her?

James thought none of these things, of course. He was glad to speak of his profession and explain it to Miss Fraser. The truth of the matter was that he never had to do this before, and he was not quite sure where to begin.

"Well, in essence, it means that clients come to me with a problem: they suspect that their wives are adulterous, or that someone is stealing from them, or they want me to find a missing person, something of the kind. And, for a fee, I apply myself and my resources to solving their problem."

Rose was intrigued by this answer, and by the possibility it presented. Perhaps...

"Forgive me, sir, but it was my impression that such matters were usually dealt with by the police."

"The police, for all their other qualities, are over-worked, underpaid and often mistrusted. Even when someone does report a crime, they must focus their resources on the cases they believe they can close. In some cases, my clients have been rejected by the police and are seeking my help to bring about justice. In other cases, the client never went to the police at all, because they didn't trust them to do their work or to be discreet enough on a matter that would bring them some embarrassment if not handled properly, or because they feared their case was too trivial to be brought to the attention of the authorities. Once I have collected enough evidence to apprehend a criminal, I turn the case over to the authorities, who do with it as they see fit."

This applied to her situation perfectly. Her 'case', as he said, was much too trivial to bring to the police. All she had were a few notes, and a feeling of dread. If Mr. Grey agreed to help, though, if he could find the man and stop him... But would she dare ask him? Would it not be too forward, on a first meeting? Of course it would be. She could not bring herself to such a bold, improper move.

"Your line of work is unusual indeed. It seems to me that you enjoy it a great deal, though."

"I do. I feel it is the duty of every man to make a difference in the world, whenever possible."

Rose would have agreed with him, and then left him in command of the conversation, for it was becoming obvious that she could not be trusted in this position, when she heard something horrible. Something so unexpected and ghastly that she would have frozen in place, were it not for Mr. Grey leading the dance.

One of the violins had screeched.

"Miss Fraser? Are you all right?"

"Did you not hear that?" she asked with incredulity.

"Hear what?" His question was answered mere moments later, when the violin screech sounded once more.

James immediately searched for the source of the horrible sound. The culprit quickly made himself obvious: not only by the wineglass perched on the stand, but by the ruddy complexion of the violinist, which betrayed that the empty glass had not been the first he consumed.

"Ah, yes. One glass too many for the poor chap, I fear."

Rose took advantage of the next turn to see what Mr. Grey meant.

"I cannot believe it. This is a ball. People are dancing. And the man providing the music is too drunk to properly handle his own instrument. How can anyone fail to see how critical it is to hire decent musicians when one is entertaining?"

James struggled to contain his untimely laughter. He was not used to seeing a young woman defend her opinions with such passion, and the argument was most uncommon as well. It was all very amusing. Miss Fraser was showing herself to be wonderful company.

Rose, on the other hand, was already regretting her outburst. A lady must check her temper at all times; her aunt had repeated the sentiment often enough, though she sometimes failed to live by it. Nobody wants a shrew for a wife. The good opinion of Mr. Grey was undoubtedly lost to her, now. The best she could hope for was to salvage something of her dignity.

"My apologies, sir. That was inappropriate."

"Not at all, Miss Fraser, I assure you. You have raised a valid point."

James did not understand the change in Miss Fraser's mood, but he knew enough of the character of women to guess that unless he could cheer her up again, their time together would end on an awkward, sour note. She would not acknowledge him again, and he would lose the chance to court her just as he was beginning to appreciate what a treasure she was.

"I'm afraid that Lady de Courcy may have exceeded her reach for this ball. The gilded dinner service must have proven to be more expensive then she had expected."

Rose would have insisted that she had been most silly, and that it was not her place to criticize the hostess, but Mr. Grey's last intervention shocked the words out of her mind.

"Gilded?" This could not be right. And yet Mr. Grey was nodding. Perhaps she misunderstood the meaning of the word. "You mean gold?"

"Covered in gold leaves, to be precise, but the end result should be the same."

"Dinner plates covered in gold?"

"And bowls as well, not to mention forks, knifes and spoons. My impression is that the viscountess wishes to make this ball, the first of the season, memorable, so that the following balls will be judged and found lacking. She must have hoped that the dinner service and the peacocks would amuse the guests sufficiently, and they would not notice the sub-par musicians."

"Peacocks?! To eat?"

James could not contain his laughter this time. "No, no." But then a thought struck him. He did not know the menu for the evening. "That is, well, I don't think so. I meant the decorations. But then again, it is possible that Lady de Courcy joined some strange epicurian club without my knowledge. We could very well be eating peacock, for all I know."

Rose had to admit, she never even saw the decorative birds, however prominently displayed they were. They were too similar to the colorful and exotic Londoners in her eyes. Mr. Grey's revelation seemed too fantastic to be true; she could not help but laugh at it.

"Eating peacock out of a gold plate, using a gold fork and a gold knife. The viscountess would have succeeded after all; how could such a thing be outdone?"

"The London season is a time of wonder, Miss Fraser. All excesses are permitted."

"I'm afraid this may be too much for a simple girl from the North."

"'Tis not so bad; a bit of cleverness and a sure hand to guide you are all you need."

He knew now that she had more than a bit of cleverness, and as for the sure hand... He was willing to offer his, should it be necessary. As their dance ended, he guided her back to Mrs. Edwards.

Once they reached her aunt, Rose turned to curtsy to Mr. Grey, who bowed to her.

"Thank you for the dance, Mr. Grey."

"The pleasure was mine, Miss Fraser." He was smiling, and she knew from their conversation that the smile and the pleasantness it portrayed were genuine. She suspected that her aunt would have much to say about the dangers of attaching yourself too closely to the first man introduced to you, but Rose could not help it: she hoped to see Mr. Grey again.

Chapter 4

The following morning, James found his mind both in the past and the future, rather than in the present. The night had brought unexpected pleasures, the main of which being the acquaintance of Miss Rose Fraser.

Of course, the term acquaintance might be considered presumptuous. She had yet to acknowledge him outside of the ballroom. His attempt to secure a more solid connection by walking the ladies back to their residence had been firmly rejected by Mrs. Edwards.

Nonetheless, he was hopeful that Miss Fraser might share his affection, and he could think of no reason for Mr. and Mrs. Edwards to refuse him the privilege of courting their niece. He was at the moment preparing his plea, which he would deliver this morning as he called on them.

He should also send a thank you note to Lady De Courcy, not only for the invitation to her ball, but also for giving him the Edwards's address. He suspected that Her Ladyship had expected him to make such a request, and that she was as happy with the turn of events as he was.

Thinking of his good luck reminded him of Cowper. They did not have the opportunity to speak for the remainder of the evening. James wondered if his friend made an impression on Lady Newport.

As he was questioning whether he should try to find Cowper in the afternoon - the man would probably be at their club - and ask him, the housekeeper announced that his father had come to visit.

What could Lord Henry possibly want with his youngest son, so early in the day? James could not say. His father was not one to drop in unannounced, unless the matter was deemed urgent.

Perhaps Lady de Courcy had paid Lord Henry a call this morning and brought up Miss Fraser. It would be somewhat presumptuous, but not at all unlike the viscountess to take the first opportunity to brag about her talents as a matchmaker. If such was the case, Lord Henry would most likely come to demand that his son give him a more detailed account of his evening, and of his intentions.

James had such a hard time imagining any other reason for his father to visit, that he was certain to have guessed the truth of the matter, though his judgment, it must be said, was ever so slightly muddled by his encounter with Miss Fraser.

He had enough wit about him, however, to realize, as soon as he saw his father, that he had guessed wrong.

"Father," greeted James politely.

"Would you care to tell me about this?" Lord Henry waved the newspaper he was holding at his son for a moment before shoving it in his hands. James cautiously unfolded it, unsure as to what his father wanted from him.

"Page eight," said Lord Henry as he started pacing around the room.

James opened to the appropriate page and quickly read through various news until he found the one most likely to have brought on his father's wrath. A Mr. Jack Perry, who had been declared guilty of the murder of Miss Esther Clark, the daughter of his employers, was set to be executed today. The article briefly reviewed the case, and mentioned James's involvement in the arrest. According to the journalist, James's investigation and his testimony during trial had been crucial to the arrest of the man.

"Ah," said James softly.

"Ah. Is that all you have to say, 'Ah'? I thought I had made my opinions on the subject plainly understood, James. I permitted that you pursue this 'investigator' business, in exchange for your word that you would not be chasing down violent criminals."

"There was no chasing down, father. I merely studied the crime scene and interrogated the man, along with every other domestic, and the masters of the house. His statement was in contradiction with that of the others, so I convinced a policeman friend of mine to search his room, with the permission of Mr. Clark. They found the condemning piece of evidence, and Perry was arrested. See, no chasing down whatsoever."

"You are not so obtuse, so don't pretend to be. You know what I mean. You agreed to take this case, knowing it was an affair of murder. If that Perry had known of your suspicions..."

"But he didn't know. Not until it was too late for him to do anything but go to jail. I was never in any danger."

"You have no way of knowing that! You should have turned those people down."

"I've been in the business less than a year; I can't afford to turn down clients."

Lord Henry could have said then that James's personal fortune, not to mention his own, more than allowed him to turn down the cases which he, as his father, did not approve of. He chose to let his snort speak for him.

"I'm still building a reputation," continued James. "You are the one who always told us that the mark of a true gentleman is that he's unafraid to work hard and earn back his privileges."

"And therefore I should rejoice that the way you choose to earn back your privilege puts your life in danger? And don't bring up your brother again!"

James sighed. It was a conversation that they had had many times before, and they could now guess what each would say next. This was indeed the point where James would bring up his brother John, who was currently a Captain in Her Majesty's Royal Army, stationed in India. If one was to believe the baron, fighting for Queen and Country was the only tolerable way to risk a son's life.

Lord Henry was pacing. James remained silent. He was waiting for his father's next line.

"If you had a family of your own, you would understand," finally declared Lord Henry, right on schedule. This would be James's cue to roll his eyes and reply 'If you say so, father.'

Instead, he said this: "Then the time of my understanding may come soon."

Lord Henry abruptly stopped pacing and turned to face his son. The two men studied each other.

"You're trying to distract me," finally replied Lord Henry. "You would not look nearly this calm if you had engrossed some girl."

James could not deny the truth of either statement. He rather chose to supply more information. "I met someone, last night, at Lady De Courcy's ball: Miss Rose Fraser. I understand that she's something of a protegé of the viscountess; a neighbor from the North."

Lord Henry's gaze didn't waver. The boy was telling the truth; he could always tell when one of his sons tried to lie to him. This declaration may have been an attempt to deviate the conversation, and as such he should ignore it and stick to the point. But for his youngest son to throw around the idea of marriage and children, even in jest, after only one meeting, the girl must be important.

If this relationship was pursued, and led to marriage, perhaps then his son would stop living so recklessly. Surely James would not put himself in danger if a family depended on him. He might even abandon this silly investigation business altogether, return to school and become a barrister. That would suit his needs for justice while keeping him safe.

And perhaps Lord Henry would stop dreading the newspaper. He would no longer need his butler to read it first, in case one of those ghastly articles would be reporting the details of his son's murder.

"I want to meet the girl," Lord Henry finally said.

"I'm sure that between you and the viscountess, something can be arranged."

Lord Henry nodded, grabbed his hat and coat, and after a quick goodbye, left the house.

James was momentarily stunned; he had not expected the distraction to work so well. His father had not even declared the usual 'This discussion is not over' on the way out.

He regained his senses and looked at his watch. Enough time had passed; the hour was now appropriate to pay a call on the Edwards and Miss Fraser.

***

"I believe a walk in the park is in order today, Rose."

"A walk, my aunt?" The declaration surprised Rose. She had presumed that the morning would be spent sifting through invitations, the number of which would no doubt increase; she had been assured of that the previous night.

"Yes, a walk. It will give us an opportunity to further our acquaintance with some of the ladies present at the ball. There was such a crowd, we hardly got a chance to speak two words to anyone, save the viscountess. If only half of those who swore to me that walking was the best form of exercise are in the park today, the morning will be most productive indeed."

Rose supposed she should be relieved that the shopping frenzy was done with, at least for now. Of course, most of the shopping had been done by carriage. But on the other hand, this excursion in the park could not last as long as an outing to the shops did.

Could it?

"I thought that the morning was the time you went through your mail."

Mrs. Edwards held back a sigh at her husband's remark. "There is more than enough time to see to this when we return," she explained patiently.

"My dear, you must forgive my intrusion in your domain. I know precious little about this affair of husband hunting. But suppose one of those missives is urgent?"

As she heard those words, Mrs. Edwards did sigh. She knew very well that no urgent missive was awaiting them, and so did her husband. But Mr. Edwards, it seemed, was determined to be difficult this morning. They were pressed for time, indeed, but arguing with him would take longer than the time necessary to go through the mail. Humoring him was the lesser evil.

"Robinson, the mail."

Robinson arrived mere moments later, with a small stack of envelopes on a silver tray. Everyone had a little bit of mail waiting for them that morning. He first gave Mr. Edwards his share, then Mrs. Edwards hers, and was placing the rest in front of Rose when someone knocked at the door. As Robinson bowed and went to see to who it was, Rose noticed the familiar, dreaded piece of folded paper.

This was about the ball, she thought, but any further speculation was interrupted by her aunt.

"Well, Rose." At these words, Rose was startled and dropped the anonymous note on her lap. "Are any of those letters marked Urgent?"

Rose flipped through her mail quickly, distracted. "No, my aunt."

Having heard the answer she expected, Mrs. Edwards turned to her husband. "Satisfied, Mr. Edwards?"

"Beyond my wildest dreams."

It was at that moment that Robinson came back and announced that Mr. James Grey had come to pay a call.

"Good morning, Mrs. Edwards, Miss Fraser. Ah, Mr. Edwards, I presume. James Grey. Nice to meet you. Say, terrible weather we're having today, isn't it?"

James bowed to the group. Mr. Edwards replied with an almost imperceptible nod. The two men stood eye to eye, and the younger man could tell that the elder was most displeased that his quiet morning had been interrupted.

Mrs. Edwards and Miss Fraser both curtsied to him, but their greeting was less than enthusiastic. Mrs. Edwards was too good at dissimulating her emotions for him to decipher them on such a short-lived acquaintance; he could only get the vaguest impression that she judged his presence to be somehow inopportune. Miss Fraser, on the other hand, looked as though she had seen a ghost. And what was she gripping so strongly in her left hand?

"Mr. Grey." Mrs. Edwards's voice interrupted his observations. "I am afraid I have no idea what you mean. The weather..."

The rest of her sentence was drowned out by the sudden thunder, and by the torrential rain which followed.

Everyone stared at James, silent and shocked. The butler was the first to regain his wits, and after a moment, he asked, "Sir, if I may, how did you..."

"How did I guess? It was nothing, really. I could feel a tingle in the back of my nose. It always happens minutes before a storm, always have, since I was a boy. They say I have my grandfather's nose. He could smell a storm from a mile away."

Mrs. Edwards invited James to sit down, and sent away for tea. Her tone was not quite gracious, though. Perhaps the poor weather had ruined previous plans, and she was still put off. Mr. Edwards, on the other hand, made no attempt at civility and marched away, having never spoken a word. What a strange, rude man!

Rose felt as though she had only half her wits about her. She realized that the rain had ruined her aunt's plans for a walk in the park, and the news should have brought her relief just as it had brought her aunt disappointment, but it did not. She knew that her uncle was being intolerably rude, and that should have embarrassed her, but it did not. She had hoped to see Mr. Grey again, and the fact that he paid her a call the morning after their first meeting should have brought her pleasure beyond belief, and yet she could not feel the joy.

She wished to be alone, so that she may read the dreadful thing by herself, and weep and fear and rage, and not risk embarrassment in front of the domestics, or her aunt and uncle, or Mr. Grey. She wished Robinson had waited five more minutes to bring the mail, that he had opened the door to Mr. Grey first. She wished that this note, and all the previous notes, had never been sent.

"Miss Fraser?"

Rose was startled to find herself on a small chair in the sitting room. Mr. Grey had taken a seat on the sofa.

They appeared to be alone, until Rose noticed her aunt at the doorway, discussing with Robinson.

"Perhaps this is a bad time. I can make my excuses if you would rather be alone and read this letter you are holding."

Rose could not help herself; she let out a laugh. A sad and cynical laugh.

"Read this letter... I assure you, Mr. Grey, I would much rather not read this at all. I could spare myself the insults and the threats. The fourth one since I came into town. The fourth one!"

Rose suddenly got up, tossing the offending note to the ground and took a few steps forward.

"Rose, what are you doing up? Sit down!"

Her aunt's admonition aborted Rose's pacing. With a sigh, she moved back toward her seat.

"Miss Fraser," James spoke up quickly, "if I may, the hem of your dress is caught. Allow me." He acted quickly, before anyone might notice that his excuse to get on the floor was not only flimsy, but false. He fiddled with the hem of Miss Fraser's dress, praying to God he wasn't offending either of the ladies, and he grabbed the small piece of paper as he got back to his seat.

"Thank you, Mr. Grey."

Miss Fraser and Mrs. Edwards sat down. Tea arrived a moment later. Mrs. Edwards questioned James on the letter he was now holding.

"Oh, this? 'Tis nothing. A bit of business correspondence. Nothing that can't wait."

"Are you sure, sir? If you wish to read it now, we would have no objection."

James knew that reading or writing letters was not something one did when one was paying a call, and thought it was peculiar that the lady of the house would encourage him to do this. But, on the other hand, his curiosity was great.

"Are you certain, Mrs. Edwards?"

"Absolutely," Mrs. Edwards insisted, and it was all the encouragement that James needed. He unfolded the paper and quickly read the three lines of text it contained.

Remember, Lady Cat, as you bewitch the town

As you purr under the stroke of their hands

The familiar gets burned with the witch

The words he read first brought a feeling of dread, which burned to fury and finally cooled into determination. This man, whoever he was, thought he could torment Miss Fraser thusly, with impunity? He would soon find out how wrong he was.

He gathered what clues he could from the note. The paper was of a good quality, a solid paper of good weight and immaculate white. The pen and ink were quality materials as well; there was no fading and no blotches. The calligraphy was careful, the syntax was perfect. Whoever wrote this letter was educated. The folding of the paper was most uncommon; who would put this kind of effort to fold a note when stuffing it in an envelope, or using a seal, would do the same?

"Is everything all right, Mr. Grey?"

James looked up to his hostess. "Yes, Mrs. Edwards. But I'm afraid I must see to this business matter sooner rather than later. 'Tis poor behavior for a guest, I realize..."

"Mr. Grey, when one is married to a business man, as I am, one understands the urgency of certain matters."

At another time, James would be questioning Mrs. Edwards's suddenly lax manners. He already suspected that she had no desire to entertain him, and was in fact glad to see him gone. But he had no time to try and understand this woman, who was in her own way as strange and as rude as her husband. He had theories to ponder and plans to formulate.

"Nevertheless, pray forgive my rudeness," he added, somewhat distractedly.

"There is nothing to forgive, sir."

"I will see you out, Mr. Grey," said Rose quietly.

She was, of course, mortified that he had read the note. He was now making his excuse and leaving her presence as fast as he could. Since her aunt just as good as dismissed him, she was certain she would not see him again.

She already regretted the impulse that made her offer to escort him out, and she fully expected him to refuse.

"Rose..." Mrs. Edwards started to say, but she was interrupted by Mr. Grey, who thanked Rose and took a step back to let her guide him out of the house.

When they were out of Mrs. Edwards's sight, he whispered to her, "This is the fourth such note you've received?"

"Yes, sir."

"How did you get the other three? How did they get in the house?"

"Our butler says a street urchin delivered them."

Mr. Grey looked as shocked by this declaration as he had been by the first reading of the note. "Really? Interesting," he added, as his expression turned pensive. After a minute or so, he spoke again, "Will you come to the viscountess's dinner party, early next week?"

"I'm afraid I haven't received an invitation."

"I'll speak to her about it. Be sure to bring the other notes with you; I'll need them to build my case."

Build his case? He was going to investigate this?

The possibility filled Rose with hope and dread. Perhaps Mr. Grey would solve this, and stop the man. Perhaps her tormentor would be angry that she turned to Mr. Grey for help, and would attempt to hurt him. Perhaps the reason she was getting those notes was so terrible that Mr. Grey would turn away from her in disgust. Any number of outcomes sprung to her mind.

"Mr. Grey!" she called out.

He turned to face her. "Yes, Miss Fraser?"

Rose searched for the words to express her anxiety, yet none came. "You don't have to do this," she finally said.

He looked perplexed. "Of course I do."

He must have felt a professional obligation. Oh, goodness! She had no idea of what his fees were.

"Mr. Grey, I'm grateful that you would wish to help me. Your professional dedication is honorable. But, sir... when we first spoke of your business... you mentioned a fee... I'm afraid..."

"Miss Fraser," Mr. Grey interrupted, taking one of Rose's hands into both of his, and looking straight into her eyes. "I cannot, in good conscience, allow this torment of yours to go on. Not when I have the means to put an end to it. Let us not talk of money, it is of no matter. You must allow me to help you. Please?"

Rose could think of nothing to say, nothing to do. She merely nodded, so faintly that another might have missed it.

"Thank you," whispered Mr. Grey.

James reluctantly let go of Miss Fraser's hand as the butler arrived to help him into his coat and hat. He bade farewell to the young lady, which some part of him already considered to be his future bride, and walked out to find a carriage. He had work to do.

Chapter 5

Mr. Grey kept his word and went to speak to Lady de Courcy that very afternoon. This proved to be an unnecessary measure: one of the letters which had arrived that morning, and been dismissed as not urgent, was an invitation, addressed to Rose and her aunt, to a small dinner party scheduled on Monday. Mr. Grey's visit to the viscountess, therefore, served no other purpose than to confirm that which she already suspected: the depth of Mr. Grey's attachment to her protégé.

Her Ladyship could barely contain her excitement. It was exactly the development she had been hoping for, and if propriety had not stopped her, she would have shouted her success as a matchmaker across the rooftops. As things stood, she had to content herself with various hints during the dinner party.

"I had hoped that the baron would be present tonight. Such a shame that his affairs kept him away. I have a feeling he would have loved to meet you, Miss Fraser, and Mrs. Edwards as well, of course."

"If I may, to whom is your Ladyship referring?" asked Aunt Edwards.

"Henry Grey, the Baron of Rotherfield. You may remember, I introduced you to his son at the ball last Thursday. The whole family are dear personal friends of mine, you know."

"Mr. Grey mentioned that you were also a good friend of his mother's," added Rose softly.

"Oh! Dear Cecilia." The viscountess's emotions at these words were plain to see. "She was an angel, nothing short of an angel, Miss Fraser. You remind me a bit of her, you know. And when she met the baron, it was love at first sight. They were married before the end of the season. The same thing happened when Albert, the eldest son, met his wife Charlotte. When the Grey men meet The One, they waste no time."

"It appears that your friend was very lucky," said one of the other guests as Her Ladyship stopped to catch her breath.

"Or unlucky," muttered Aunt Edwards, keeping her eyes firmly on her niece.

"Unlucky? Mrs. Edwards, how can you say so?"

"It seems a shame to me that the baron's late wife had to suffer an aborted season because her suitor was too eager. I can think of no reason why they could not wait until the end of the season to marry."

"Well, I can think of no reason why they should have waited. And I'll let you know, Mrs. Edwards, that Cecilia's season was in no way aborted. A young bride can enjoy the season just as a debutante might. And even more, I should say; she doesn't have the pressure of husband hunting."

Mrs. Edwards, who now understood how she was insulting the viscountess, wisely dropped the subject.

Rose could not help but wonder what had possessed her aunt to antagonize Lady de Courcy so. It seemed to her that her aunt was trying to convey a message.

A young bride can enjoy the season, but she has no need of a chaperon. Rose knew that if not for the generosity of the viscountess, she would have had no way to enter the prestigious London society. And Aunt Edwards would have no access to said society without Rose.

The young woman was expected to marry, that much had been made clear from the start. But what Rose was only now noticing was that her aunt would be much displeased should an engagement be announced before August.

On the other hand, there was the genuine danger to her reputation. Rose knew little of Mr. Grey's business, but she imagined that they would have to meet regularly, especially if she was to hand him not only the notes in her possession, but also those that she may receive in the future. If they were seen too often together, people would start to talk. If those meetings were not soon followed with a public engagement, she could very well be ruined. And even with the engagement, the time she and Mr. Grey could spend together would be limited, and heavily chaperoned. Rose suspected that it would not do, and she resolved to mention this to Mr. Grey. Hopefully he would have thought of this first and devised a plan.

***

James, as a matter of fact, had done no such thing. The idea that meeting Miss Fraser frequently could potentially be damaging to her reputation had not crossed his mind, an oversight he now dearly regretted. Dinner was over, and the company had retired for cards and conversation. James had taken the opportunity to sit next to Miss Fraser, and they were now discussing in a low voice. He could only hope that they were avoiding undue attention.

"You are correct, Miss Fraser. A plan must be devised. Allow me to consider the matter for a moment. Meanwhile, may I have the previous notes?"

After a quick look around, Miss Fraser passed him three folded squares of paper. "I hope you don't mind. I thought that re-folding them would make it simpler to give them to you. I'm afraid I've done a poor job of it."

"It was clever of you, and I'm sure you did a wonderful job. May I inquire as to the times and dates you received each of these?"

"Well, I received the first one the very day I arrived in town. It was delivered during dinner. The second last Monday, it was waiting for me with the rest of the mail when I returned from shopping. And the third on Wednesday evening, after my uncle, my aunt and I returned from dinner with some old friends."

James took the information with a pensive nod. The beginning of a plan was forming in his mind.

"Are you in the habit of walking in the park?"

"Um, yes, my aunt and I go almost every morning, at nine. Sir, arranging to meet in the park would not be a solution. The place is very crowded, you know. We would be noticed."

"Miss Fraser, I must ask two things of you. First, should you receive any further communication from this man, kindly put it in your reticule when you go walking. Second, please, have a little faith in me. I believe I now have a plan."

They were interrupted by the dealer reminding Miss Fraser that it was her turn to play, and they did not speak of the matter again. At the end of the current game, James took his leave. He had an errand to run the next day, if his deductions were correct. He would require a great deal of luck, but should that errand be successful, it would allow him to pursue his investigation while protecting Miss Fraser's reputation.

***

Tuesday evening, James found himself on Charles Street once more. This time, however, he did not walk up to the Edwards residence. Rather, he stood about ten yards away, waiting for a messenger, and hoping he had not already missed him. Assuming, of course, that the messenger existed at all.

After all, the only person who had seen this supposed urchin messenger was the butler, and he could - or would - not give any more details. It would be foolish not to consider the possibility that the boy did not exist. Perhaps the butler was covering for another servant, or for a more important man. Perhaps it was all a ruse, and the butler wrote the notes himself.

James had been waiting for nearly an hour when he noticed a small boy covered in rags. The sleeves of his coat were pushed up past his elbows, and his hands and arms were so clean, the contrast with the rest of his person was almost painful. He held something in his hands, at a careful distance from his body, and slowly made his way up the street, looking around in confusion, as if he did not know exactly where he was, or where he was going.

The boy eventually made his way to the Edwards front door and knocked. The door opened. The butler sneered as the boy presented what James could now see was a folded piece of paper. The boy ran off as soon as the butler had closed his hands on the paper. James followed him, taking care to keep his distance and not be noticed.

The boy led him on a merry chase, before disappearing in one of the seedier neighborhoods of London, as was to be expected. Placing a hand to the small of his back, James took a minute to catch his breath, and readjust his clothes.

Things had gone as well as could be expected. He not only confirmed to himself the existence of the messenger; he discovered his dwelling and ascertained that he was but one of many. Had he made the delivery before, the boy would have been more confident as to the location of the house. James also suspected that the other delivery boys also lived nearby. It would only be logical that whoever hired these boys chose them all in the same neighborhood, rather than traipsing around all over the city.

James had made a small dent in what was the biggest obstacle in this investigation: lack of information. To make an even bigger one, which he intended to do, he would need help.

A few options presented themselves to him. The most obvious would be to find the young boy who had led him here, since he was, as far as James knew, the only person who had seen Miss Fraser's tormentor with his own eyes. But this solution presented several problems, the first being that the young boy might have been threatened or bribed into secrecy, and the second being that young boys living on the street usually belonged to gangs, and the men who led these gangs usually had very strict control over the boys' time and movements.

He considered sending a trusted servant to observe the area and report to him, and rejected the idea immediately. His most trusted servants would stand out in the area, as much as he did himself. Besides, they could miss important details.

He needed someone who really knew this place, someone who lived here. Someone observant, who would have already noticed the man who came at least five times in the last fortnight to hire youths as delivery boys. Most importantly, James needed someone he could trust.

As he took another look around, getting a sense of the people surrounding him, he noticed the boy. Not the one he had been chasing: this one was older, about fifteen, maybe. He was tall for his age, and dressed a little better than the rest of the crowd. He walked with confidence toward James, an arrogant smirk on his face.

This boy looked promising.

"Hello, stranger," said the boy once he had reached James's side. His voice was settled, and lower then James had expected. Perhaps the boy was older than fifteen after all. His eyes, slightly too big for his head, and his cleanly shaved face, gave an impression of youth that might have been misleading. "You lost?"

"Perhaps. Would you be in a position to help me if I was?"

"Could be. But this place here ain't ideal, right? Pretty noisy, too many people. How 'bout we go find someplace more... private, to talk?"

"Lovely idea. I could use a meal, and a bit of rest."

"Well, then, you're in luck, stranger. I know just the place."

The boy took James by the arm and guided him to a nearby house. As they were about to cross the threshold, James felt a prickle on the left side of his back, an inch or so above the belt.

It appeared that Lady Luck was smiling down on him. This was simply perfect.

They both walked into the house, the boy ahead. After a short walk across a closet-sized vestibule, the first floor opened up into the main room. It was set up as some kind of sitting room, but James simply could not bring himself to use that term to describe this room. It was a pub with no tables, and even that description was generous.

The room was largely unoccupied. A small group of men were sitting together, engaged in a low discussion over pints of beer. Two other men were sitting apart from the group and from each other, reading newspapers.

There was only one woman in the room; she was serving the group of men. She looked just the part of the owner of lodging quarters. She was the right age, and looked stern and proper, even though she was obviously lower middle class.

She looked up at them, sighed, and walked up to her two new visitors, grabbing the youngest one by the arm and dragging him back to the vestibule.

"Penny, my love!"

"You need to leave," Penny said.

"But we just got here. My friend and I need a room for a little while."

"And I need to not get in trouble. One of us is going to be disappointed, and it won't be me."

"Ah, come now, Penny. When have I ever been trouble?"

"William Vaughn, I've known you since you were this high, and you've never been anything BUT trouble."

"Excuse me," interrupted James. He got down on one knee and reached inside his shoe. "I have rather important business to discuss with this young man, privately," he said as he straightened up, holding a five pounds note. "I hope that this will suffice to assuage your fears, along with my word that no one here will get in any trouble."

Penny took the offered note suspiciously. When she saw that it was an official note, printed at the Bank of London, her hands shook. She was used to being paid in shillings and pennies. She couldn't remember the last time she held that much money in her hands at one time, if ever.

"Is this for real?" she finally asked.

"Yes, madam."

She eyed James warily for a minute longer. Something in his attitude must have convinced her that he was telling the truth, because she eventually tucked the note inside her sleeve. It was in most probability the safest place for it.

"Well, hmm, would you like to get some supper in your room? I have some stew, and a bit of cheese and bread."

"That would be wonderful. Thank you very much." James was now the one holding the boy, William Vaughn, by the arm. William was studying James, trailing his gaze down to his shoes and back to his eyes, looking curious, but also cautious. The sign of a good brain.

"Well, then. Follow me." Penny turned around, leading James and William to their room.

Once they were left alone, James pulled a handkerchief and dabbed his back, where he had felt the prickle earlier. "You may give back the purse you took from me," he said to William. "I do not care about the rocks I used to fill it, but the purse itself has a sentimental value."

William, confused, took his stolen goods out of his pocket and examined them. The purse was indeed filled with many small rocks, and one of the straps was pierced through with something.

"What... Is that a needle?"

"Of course! How else am I supposed to know that someone is stealing from me?" James shoved his handkerchief back into his pocket. "I expected more blood, however. You must have gotten the angle just right. You're good. I also expected you to wait until we were in the room to try and take it. Why pick my pocket in the streets?"

William was very confused. After a moment, he said, "I've got to tell you, stranger, of all the queer folk I've met in my life, you take the cake."

"Possibly. You haven't answered my question."

The boy stared at James in disbelief for a few more seconds, and then shrugged. "Let's just say, I've learned from experience to get paid as early as possible in the transaction."

"Aren't you afraid someone would call the police?"

"They've got more to lose then I do," answered William, with a cocky grin.

"Yes, I suppose you're right about that. Anyway, down to business. I have a proposition for you."

The boy scoffed. "Oh, yeah? What else is new?"

"Not that kind of proposition. I am hoping to locate someone."

This news did not please William at all. "A bobby!" he spit out between curses. "I should have known. If you think I'm selling out anyone..."

"Calm down, young man. I'm not a policeman. A private party hired me to locate this man, whom I'm pretty sure is unknown to you. He showed up in this neighborhood many times, at least five, maybe more, but he doesn't live here. About a fortnight ago, he started hiring young boys to deliver messages. He makes them wash their hands first."

William looked at James dubiously. "So? What does it have to do with me?"

"That depends on you."

Sharp knocks sounded from the other side of the door. James opened it and found Penny carrying their dinner on a tray. He took the tray from her with warm thanks, and set it on the bedside table.

"I believe that you know the man I'm talking about, that you've noticed him around here, and I would like you to tell me what you know."

"What if I don't know anything?"

"Do you?"

"Maybe I do, maybe I don't. Maybe I just don't want to talk to you."

"That is entirely your choice. If you decide not to talk to me, I will leave. You will have the room and dinner, paid for, to yourself, and tomorrow you can go back to scrounging, stealing and seducing enough to get you through the next day."

William appeared surprised to get so much for free. Getting something for nothing was, after all, an unusual concept. "And if I do talk?" he finally asked.

"In that case, I would give you my address and employ you."

"You mean you'll give me a job? What kind of job?"

"Observing and reporting back to me, mostly, along with a few favors. For that, you would be given a room and a meal at my house, as often as you wish or need, and a reasonable salary, open to negotiation."

William was still hesitating. He grabbed a piece of bread and started chewing on it, slowly. He swallowed that first bite before asking the question weighing most heavily on his mind: "Why me?"

"You are old enough to be independent and know how to take care of yourself. You aren't just a pickpocket, although it is certainly one of your skills. You engage with the people you target, which I suspect allowed you to develop your sense of observation and your ability to judge people at a glance. Beyond that, you were at the right place, at the right time."

William nodded to himself, picked up one of the bowls of stew and started eating. It was starting to get dark outside, and James was not looking forward to making his way through this neighborhood at night. The thought made him impatient.

"Well, William, what do you say?"

"First of all, the name's Will."

"Very well, Will. I'm Mr. Grey."

Will extended his hand to James. "All right, Mr. Grey; you've got yourself a spy." The two men shook on it. Will started eating again.

"So yeah, I've seen the guy," he reported to James in between bites. "I'm pretty sure that it's the right guy, anyway."

"What does he look like?"

"He's tall. About your height I'd say, but fatter than you. He's old, too. His hair is almost all the way gray. He's rich, dresses fancy with his shoes shined and his gloves. Talked to him once, actually."

"Did you?"

"Yeah, you know, a rich guy in this place, looking at the boys. He walked up to me, matter of fact, asked me if I was interested in making some money. He's obviously not the type, but sometimes they like to experiment, you know? And anyway, he might have had something worth taking on him. So I do my thing. He slaps me across the face! I fell down, he hit me so hard!"

"You didn't see that coming?"

"No way! You think I would try to get on with a guy who would hit me? I'm not that desperate. He looked like the normal snob, looking down his nose at the little people, and then he went insane. The worst part is, he took off his gloves and threw them on the ground in front of me, with that look of disgust on his face. Like touching me made them so dirty they were unwearable."

"I don't suppose you still have the gloves?"

"Never had them. Someone else ran up and grabbed them. And even if I'd thought to take them, I probably would have sold them a long time ago. But seriously, Mr. Grey, I think that guy is real bad news."

"I suspected as much, but I still need to find him."

"But, well, I won't have to get too close to him, or talk to him, will I?"

Will looked so genuinely scared of this man, it made him appear younger than ever. "Don't worry, you won't," reassured James as best he could. "Seeing and not being seen is what I expect of you."

"Along with those favors you talked about."

"Yes, in fact, thank you for reminding me. I need you to do the first of those favors tomorrow."

James grabbed one of his calling cards from his breast pocket and put it on the table. He had expected to find a small pencil there as well, but he did not. He was patting himself around, trying to find it, when Will's voice distracted him.

"The...Honorable...James...Frederick...Henry Grey." The boy was peering down at James's card, his voice hesitant as he painstakingly deciphered every word. "Is that you?" he asked, looking back at James.

"Yes, it is. I didn't realize you could read."

"Penny taught me. I was always in the kitchen, begging for food, making a pest of myself. One day, she says she'll only feed me if I sit quietly in a corner and read. I can't read that fancy, curly stuff, but you know, regular letters, like in the newspaper, those are all right."

"Excellent! This makes thing much easier." James finally found his pencil, took his card again from Will, and carefully printed out his address before giving it back. "This is my address. Can you find this place by yourself?"

Will's face lit up when he recognized the street name. "Oh yeah, no problem."

"Good." James pulled out another card, and wrote a note in cursive on the back of it. "Tomorrow, at nine, I need you to go to Hyde Park."

***

The next morning, when she came back from her walk in the park, Rose made her excuses to her aunt and ran up to her bedroom. She had been struggling with her curiosity for hours, and she was fast losing the battle. She needed to know what her latest note said. It was bad enough that she never read the one before the last, the one Mr. Grey took when he paid her a morning call.

She opened her reticule and reached for the note she had placed there before leaving the house, and found in its stead the calling card of The Honorable James Frederick Henry Grey. On the back was written:

Miss Fraser, I hope that this means of obtaining the notes from you satisfies your need for discretion. Until we meet again, I remain your faithful servant.

Chapter 6

And so the days passed. Rose did not speak to Mr. Grey, though they did see each other when she accompanied her aunt to the opera on Thursday. Those few moments of eye contact had been worth the snide comments that her aunt had taken to make whenever Mr. Grey was seen, or mentioned in conversation.

No new note arrived on Friday, which should have been a greater relief than it was. Rose had come to believe that her tormentor could read her mind, and that he would have had a few choice words about her feelings for Mr. Grey. She could not quite convince herself otherwise, despite the lack of note as evidence.

On Saturday morning, at breakfast time, the plans for what had become the usual walk in the park were dashed by an apologetic Robinson.

"Oh, for Heaven's sake!" exclaimed Aunt Edwards after Robinson gave her an extensive list of household affairs that required her attention. "Can you not take care of this yourself?"

"I've managed what I can, madam, but I'm afraid these matters do require your attention."

"This will take me all morning. But if there is no other choice... Rose, you will find some other way to busy yourself this morning. Try not to get in anyone's way."

"I could take you to the park, if you still wish to go."

Everyone turned to look at Uncle Edwards, who simply finished his breakfast, apparently unaware of the shock his words had caused.

"You? Walk in the park?" Aunt Edwards laughed at the idea.

"Of course I would not walk," replied Uncle Edwards, offended by the suggestion. "We would take the horse and carriage, go for a ride."

"Oh, you are being ridiculous, my dear. You have not handled a carriage since we left for the city."

"Exactly, and high time I got back to it. And it seems to me that, as you'll undoubtedly be busy this morning, the decision belongs to Rose."

When both her aunt and uncle turned to her, Rose was reminded of the dinner conversation that preceded their departure for London, these many nights ago. This time, however, the decision came much more swiftly. She had missed her uncle; his company, which had always been easier for her to bear, had been scarce since their arrival in town. Her aunt would be very busy this morning. Besides all that, it was a beautiful day, and it would be a shame to spend it cooped up inside.

"I think a carriage ride in the park is a wonderful idea. I would love to."

"Excellent! Then the matter is resolved. We leave in half an hour."

As her aunt had no real objections to the scheme, thus ended the discussion.

***

"Now that we are alone," said Uncle Edwards as the horse and carriage made its way down the street and to the park, "how are you, Rose?"

"I am well, uncle."

"I assume that by 'well', you mean your aunt hasn't run you completely ragged yet." Her uncle sighed. "Rose, I wish you would stand up for yourself. The world will not end if you say no to her."

"She would be upset with me, uncle. You know how I dislike conflict of any kind."

"Conflict is a part of life, my dear. You will never be able to please everyone you meet at all times. Tell me, honestly, do you enjoy life in the city so far? Shopping and walks in the park and dance lessons, every morning? Calling on a different person for tea every afternoon, followed by dinners and evenings at the theaters and balls, every night?"

"It is somewhat tiring, I must admit."

"We both know where this is leading, if your aunt has any say over this: you married to the richest man you can sink your teeth into, so you can keep on this crazy merry-go-round social scene. Is this what you want?"

"No," said Rose hesitantly.

"But..."

"I do not wish for the richest man, but for a good man. One who would care for me. One who, perhaps, would be agreeable to partake in a much less active role in society."

Her uncle remained silent as they entered the park, and for a moment longer still. "Would I be wrong in guessing that you already met such a man?" he finally said.

Rose quietly shook her head. "At least I hope I have."

"That boy who paid a call on you last week. What was his name, Grey?"

Rose nodded. Her uncle nodded as well, seemingly lost in thought.

Rose could not explain what happened next. It felt like something out of a nightmare. The horse inexplicably took off at neck-breaking speed. Her uncle cried out various interjections to the beast, to no avail. The reins, much too slack to begin with, kept slipping through his hands. The shouts of indignation of the passersby turned to cries of fear and pain, as not everyone could get out of the way in time.

Every time the carriage hit something, whether it was a person or a mere bump on the road, Rose was terribly jostled. After a particularly bad hit, she found herself thrown halfway out of the carriage. She watched helplessly as her hat fell to the ground, to be crushed under the carriage wheel. She feared her head would be next.

It was at that moment that Uncle Edwards took back the reins and violently pulled the carriage to a stop. It was too much for Rose's precarious position, and she fell.

Thankfully, she was saved from a painful landing by a pair of strong hands, who gripped her arm and awkwardly pulled her back in the carriage.

"Are you hurt?"

There was something familiar about the voice, though she was certain she never heard it before. She looked up at her savior: the man was indeed a complete stranger.

"Miss?" the stranger asked again as he tried to catch his breath. Rose realized that she has not answered his question. She shook her head: she was scared but unharmed.

"I believe that was enough excitement for today," said Uncle Edwards. "Let's go home."

"Would you allow me to accompany you? It appears that your horse is easily startled; you may find yourself in need of assistance again."

"We are much obliged to you, sir, but that won't be necessary. We reside nearby, and I'll be keeping a better grip on the reins from now on."

"Very well, if you insist, I'll let you be on your way. Good day, sir."

Uncle Edwards tilted his hat to the man and awkwardly turned the carriage around.

***

"Oh, Goodness. What have you done with yourselves? Where is your hat, Rose?" Aunt Edwards fussed over Rose's disheveled hair and dress as soon as she stepped into the vestibule. Uncle Edwards had left her at the door, declaring that he needed a drink and was headed to the pub.

"Something scared the horse, and the carriage went out of control. I am afraid I lost my hat in the incident."

It would have been ungenerous of Mrs. Edwards to take pleasure in her husband's failure to control the horse and carriage he insisted on taking out this morning. And yet what else could explain the satisfied smile that graced her face, if only for a moment?

"Well, I suppose it could be worse. You are not injured, are you?"

"No, my aunt."

"Good. You will have to change for today, but with a careful pressing, the dress will be as good as new. We shall go shopping for a new hat, soon. Go to your room; I will have Eliza join you to redo your hair and help you change."

Aunt Edwards turned and made her way out of the vestibule, with Rose at her heels. The very next moment, the door opened and Robinson walked in.

"Robinson?" Rose had not expected him to be out. "Where have you been?"

"The grocer, miss."

Rose looked down at the butler's empty hands. Before she could question him, her aunt called out. "Rose, how many times do I have to ask you to stop pestering Robinson? Go on to your room, you have to change and get your hair fixed before we leave for tea."

Rose did as her aunt bade, but questions and suspicions swarmed in her head like bees. It appeared most irregular to her for him to return from the grocer empty handed. But on the other hand, Robinson should have no need to lie to her about something so trivial. There might be a simple explanation. Perhaps he had not found what he was looking for. But Aunt Edwards had been present, and she was not one to let such an oversight go by without comment. It was possible that she didn't want to embarrass him in front of Rose, but her aunt was not usually so discreet.

She continued to question and suspect and doubt herself and others all through the day. Her feelings were only exacerbated when another note was delivered to her that evening.

Would you choose the pleasures of the city

Over your own life?

I believe this morning's event made it clear

That you cannot have both

Her tormentor had scared the horse into running off, then. He could have killed her. He probably would kill her, unless she left London, which she could not do.

This confirmation of her worst fears was not as terrible as the possibility that this tormentor was much closer than she had believed, that perhaps he lived under the same roof. This possibility, Rose could neither fully accept nor reject. She slept poorly that night.

Chapter 7

Rose had been a lot more nervous at the idea of getting in a carriage, any carriage, since the incident on Saturday morning. She realized that the fear was somewhat irrational; if her beliefs were true, and it was her tormentor who had scared the horse in an attempt to scare, injure, or even kill her, then he would be foolish to use the same technique two days in a row.

Still, she was trembling when she entered the berline, the vehicle her aunt insisted was necessary for this journey. It was much sturdier than the small carriage her uncle had driven the previous day, though, which reassured her. It would be next to impossible for Rose and her aunt to fall out of the carriage, as it was essentially a closed box. The driver and the footman would not have the same luck should something happen, since their position forced them to remain outside of the box.

Such things, however, were out of her control. And she could do nothing but grip the edge of her seat and pray for a safe journey.

She let out a small sigh of relief when they reached their destination: Smiths Hall, where they have been invited to spend the afternoon. She was sad to see that Mr. Grey was not among the guests, but noticed Mary Jones's presence with pleasure.

The weather held on, though a thin layer of clouds dimmed the sunlight. Therefore, outdoors activities were planned. Tea was served on the lawn, children flew kites, carriage rides were planned for later in the afternoon, and a lane of bowls was drawn up. There was also a separate area, where a strange new game was being played.

"Mr. Hunter insisted," explained their hostess, Mrs. Hunter. "We just returned from Leamington, you see. While we were there, we met a Major Gem, who had been working on this new game. From what I understand, it is a mixture of a French game and a Spanish one. It is called lawn racquet, and Mr. Hunter took a particular liking to it. He must play the game whenever the weather is nice."

The game, aside from being strange, seemed to involve a lot of physical activity. The players were all running around the field, hitting a ball with a racquet. The game was mostly played by the gentlemen, though a few of the younger ladies asked to be taught.

Rose would not have been one of these women, even if, by some miracle, she had not been chaperoned by her aunt of the very strong opinions. "A lady does not over exert herself, in any manner. The only acceptable exception is to dance too much at a ball, and even that should be avoided if at all possible by sitting out every third dance."

While the "every third dance" rule seemed arbitrary, Rose was grateful for it. Her stamina could not bear more than two dances without resting. She was not an active person, and in fact lacked any sort of ability for sports. She had been known to be thrown off a trotting horse. Her archery skills were nonexistent. And when her hosts insisted that she play one game of bowls, her poor aim was a source of amusement for all. One or two of the bolder gentlemen offered their help, until they were scared off by her aunt. Rose therefore kept as great a distance as she could between herself and the lawn racquet area, and she looked at the young ladies who dared approach it with a great deal of bafflement.

One of those young ladies was Mary Jones. Rose noticed her friend's presence in this section of the lawn with little surprise; Mary had always been more active and adventurous than Rose. She did not pay much attention to Mary, until she began to hear the things their hostess and other female guests were saying about her. They spoke of her with much disdain, and made many disparaging comments. Rose, who could not explain this animosity, observed Mary's acts and attitude more carefully.

What she observed was very strange. Mary spent a great deal of time with the gentlemen. She smiled and laughed a lot, giving them praise at every turn, making them laugh whenever she could. She did not blush or protest when one of the men wrapped his arms around her with the excuse of showing her how to hold and swing the racquet. Her hands often flew to their shoulders, or to her breasts. Rose was no expert on the matter, but even an amateur such as herself could tell that Mary was flirting with these men. The blatant disregard for social convention would be enough to earn the disdain of many society ladies, but Mary had taken things much further than that, and in fact, much too far: the men she was flirting with were all married.

Rose remembered the conversation she and Mary had had at that dinner party not so long ago. Mary had made an allusion to relationships that did not end in marriage, relationships where marriage was not even the intent. Rose had suspected then that Mary was considering an affair, but had rejected the idea; Mary was too smart to throw away what little security she had in life. Her family would not be able to support her in such a scandal, not with her father's political career to consider. She would be shunned, rejected by everyone who knew her, and would entirely depend on the mercy of her lover. Intelligence aside, Mary was much too independent to take such a risk; that was the reason she refused to consider marriage in the first place.

And yet, there she was, blatantly playing for the affection of married men, flaunting her lack of propriety in front of the guests, including the men's wives.

Watching her friend exhibit herself thusly made Rose feel ill. When Mary and Rose found themselves alone, it was that feeling that made her speak up.

"What in the name of God has possessed you?" Rose asked before the first pleasantry could be exchanged.

Mary, taken by surprise, could think of no better response than "What?"

"You know very well what, Mary Jones. Are you not ashamed of yourself? Those are married men!"

Mary had regained enough of her spirits to roll her eyes. "I know they are married. That is the point."

"The point? To embarrass yourself with this disgraceful behavior? Do you not feel any kind of compassion for what those poor women must be feeling, forced to watch this spectacle as it unfolds right under their noses? And your parents! What must your parents be feeling?"

"Firstly, to say that I'm embarrassing myself would mean that I feel shame in my actions, and I do not.

Secondly, I care about the feelings of these women exactly as much as their husbands do. I'm not the only one putting on a show here, I'll remind you. Thirdly and lastly, I have every reason to believe that my parents are very happy with my choices."

"Are you deranged?"

"Not at all. They are the ones who insist that I need a male protector, no matter which method I use to convince them otherwise. This should thrill them."

"You know very well that your parents meant a husband. A lover is not a protector, he has no obligation toward you."

"Neither does a husband have any obligation toward his wife."

"The husband at least has the pressure of society, the moral obligation. If a husband abandons a wife, she will have friends and family to help her. If you go on with this mad scheme of yours, you will be all alone when your lover abandons you for another convenient mistress."

"Don't worry, Rose, dearest. I have no intention of being abandoned. Once I've chosen my protector, I intend to keep him. Don't look so shocked! I assure you, it's nothing so difficult. Simply a matter of giving him what he wants while leaving him wanting for more. The newly married women my mother insisted I be introduced to were very useful in that matter."

Rose took a deep breath to try and calm herself, when a thought occurred to her. "Is this some kind of bluff? A way to shock your parents into paying to send you to medical school, or whatever it is that caught your fancy this time?"

"It started out that way, to be perfectly honest," admitted Mary with no shame. "But the more I've thought about it, the better the idea seemed. Although I would much rather be able to go out on my own and do as I will, without having to bother with a man, having to constantly flatter them does get irritating, after a while. What I wouldn't give to have your secret admirer! You are in a position to get everything you could ever want, without giving up anything at all, and you simply won't use it!"

Rose wanted to tell Mary that she was more than welcome to the man she called an admirer. Rose would have been glad to rid herself of the nauseating fear that was harder to shake every day. It would be a relief to never have to read another one of those horrible notes again. She would be thrilled to no longer have to wonder how a stranger could hate her so, or if perhaps someone she knew had hidden this hatred from her for so long that he could no longer bear it.

But before she could even attempt to find the words, she was called away by her aunt. Rose did not say farewell to Mary, did not promise to talk to her again soon. She simply walked away.

***

The rest of the afternoon was spent quietly, and, as the sun slowly disappeared below the horizon, Rose and her aunt were making their way back to town. Aunt Edwards kept herself occupied on the long ride back home by judging the quality of their hosts and of the other guests, and evaluating the boon, or the damage, this outing gave to Rose's reputation.

Rose, troubled as she was by the discovery she had made that afternoon and by the events of the previous day, was a bit slower than usual in agreeing with her aunt; however, luckily for her, Mrs. Edwards did not notice.

Mrs. Edwards interrupted herself when she noticed that the carriage was rolling to a stop, as they were nowhere near their residence at the time.

She knocked on the wall of the berline, trying to get the driver's attention. "What is going on?"

"The road's blocked by a fire engine, madam."

The sight of a fire engine was rare enough that neither Rose nor her aunt could resist a peek through the curtains.

"It's one of those weird horseless engines from America. I don't like them." The driver had to express his discontent quite loudly to be heard above the racket of the engine. "They call them combustion engines, you know? Bet there's a reason for that, and it's not good."

"They just run in the house, like that?" Rose watched the firefighters rush into the burning house, in their big, dirty uniforms, some carrying axes, some pulling a hose behind them.

"They got to, to put out the fire. Wouldn't want another Great One, would we?"

"I only see smoke." Besides, Rose could not imagine that her aunt would let anyone just run into her house that way, clearly intending to do some damage, fire or not.

"You know what they say, Miss Rose: where there's smoke, there's fire. The flames are probably deeper in the house, I'd say."

Aunt Edwards was already bored with all of this. "Can you not turn around and find another route to take us home, or will we be forced to stay here until this circus is done?"

"Yes madam."

As the driver slowly turned the carriage around, Aunt Edwards turned her attention back to the party, or, more specifically, the guests, and, most specifically, Mary Jones.

"That girl is turning wild, Rose. I do not want to see you talking to her again. If you do not keep your distance from her right now, she will bring you down with her, mark my words. I am sure that is not what you want."

"No, my aunt, it is not."

"Good. Then the matter is settled."

"Yes, my aunt." Indeed, the matter was settled. For as strange and arbitrary as her aunt's rules might appear to her, Rose knew well that, in this instance, she was right.

Chapter 8

It had been a month ago that Rose and the Edwards first came to London. Three weeks ago, she had been introduced to Mr. Grey. Since that first ball, it appeared to Rose that her patroness, Viscountess Latimer, had been endlessly scheming to introduce the Edwards family to the Grey family. What Rose didn't know was that the viscountess was not alone in her efforts. Mr. Grey's father, the Baron of Rotherfield, was as eager to meet the girl who had caught his youngest son's eye as the viscountess was to introduce them.

After three weeks of hopes and frustrations, the moment had finally arrived. On the morning in question, the Edwards received an invitation to dinner at the London residence of the Baron of Rotherfield.

The invitation was not unexpected, by any means. That is not to say that anticipation lessened the feelings accompanying the event. Rose was thrilled at the idea of meeting Mr. Grey's family, terrified that they might find her unworthy somehow, and, above all, eager to see Mr. Grey once more.

Mr. and Mrs. Edwards were not as pleased as their niece. Though neither would admit it, they both believed that the courtship of Rose and Mr. Grey was much too hasty, and that this significant step would do no good for the matter. However, one simply did not refuse an invitation to dinner from a baron.

Rose and her aunt had visited many grand houses in the last month, but the home of Lord Henry Grey had something grander still. Perhaps it was that the auspiciousness of the occasion colored their judgment, but nonetheless, Rose suddenly found herself grateful for the impromptu shopping trip her aunt had organized for them. She was at least confident that she looked her best.

Rose was also grateful that, the baron had, wisely, invited Viscountess Latimer to join this intimate dinner party.

"Miss Fraser! What a pleasure to see you this evening! Come, I must introduce you to Albert and Charlotte."

A surprise was awaiting Rose and her uncle in the sitting room. The man who stood up to meet them, the eldest son of the baron, was not quite the stranger they had expected him to be.

"Mr. Edwards and Mrs. Edwards, Miss Fraser, allow me to introduce to you Lord Albert, and his wife, Lady Charlotte."

"It is a pleasure to formally make your acquaintance, Mr. Edwards, Miss Fraser. I trust that the circumstances are better now than they were when we first met."

Mr. Edwards simply nodded politely at Lord Albert, while Rose confessed that indeed, they were. The opposite would have been almost impossible, for Lord Albert was the man who had caught her as she almost fell out of the carriage, that fateful morning in the park.

James listened as his brother and Miss Fraser explained their previous acquaintance, at the request of both the viscountess and Mrs. Edwards. When his brother had told him about the out of control carriage he had encountered in the park, and about the young girl he had rescued on that occasion, he had pressed him for as many details as possible. The note that Will had taken from Miss Fraser the next morning was wrapped in another note, from Miss Fraser herself, detailing as much as she could remember about the accident.

Which, as it turned out, was more than what Albert could remember. The sum total of his older brother's advice was to leave the matter to the police, and stay as far out of it as possible. "You know how this investigation business of yours upsets Father," Albert had said.

James might have hoped for better, but in the end he got exactly what he expected.

The pre-dinner conversation was all small talk. From the incident of Miss Fraser and Mr. Edwards, it moved on to other park activities, and open air concerts were mentioned. The subject of music kept the party talking comfortably for a while, before moving on to dance and balls and fashion. James contributed when he could, and, more often than not, he was graced with a few words from Miss Fraser in return.

By the time dinner was served, the conversation was stagnating. The seating arrangements did not help the matter. The baron was sitting at one end of the table, the viscountess at the other. The Edwards kept Rose in between them, while Lord Albert, Lady Charlotte and Mr. Grey sat across from them.

The baron, ever the gracious host, strove to find a suitable topic of discussion. His perseverance paid off: the conversation started anew when he asked uncle Edwards about his business. As the subject was one he felt comfortable with, his whole attitude became more pleasant, as did the dinner party.

With the table cleared after the last course, the men retired to the baron's study for brandy and cigars, while the women took tea and claret in the parlor. Lady De Courcy rushed to seat herself beside Aunt Edwards and engaged her in a fervent discussion of the latest on-dits. Aunt Edwards followed along and participated as best she could; she did not want to bring on the wrath of her niece's patroness, but even more than that, she was desperate not to let her ignorance of the shared gossip show.

With no other options, Rose turned her attention to Lady Grey. She was so nervous, so eager to make a good impression; she had an idea that could at least start the conversation, if she was right. It would show that she was observant and clever, a worthy companion for Mr. Grey. But, if she was wrong, she would make an utter fool of herself.

If she waited much longer, the opportunity would be lost. She took a short breath and asked: "De quelle région de France venez-vous?"

Oh, how horrible! Her pronunciation was atrocious. Her French tutor would have cringed, as he always used to do. And she could only hope that her grammar was correct.

Rose's doubts and self-recriminations all but vanished at Lady Grey's expression: it was all wonder and astonishment. "Comment avez-vous deviné?»

«Vous avez... You have a slight accent. I'm sorry, milady; I don't know the word for slight in French."

"In this context, the proper word would be léger. But I assure you, Miss Fraser, it is quite all right. It was lovely to hear someone speak in French to me again. When I first came to your country, all I heard was: 'You need to learn English. How will you learn if everyone speaks to you in French?' Not that anyone ever did."

"Does your family not speak to you in French?"

It was obvious that the question brought a great deal of sadness to Lady Grey. "Not for many years. You asked me earlier which part of France I came from. I come from a region called Alsace. Does that name mean anything to you?"

Rose slowly shook her head. The negative answer did not appear to surprise Lady Grey. "I assumed as much. England is busy enough with the wars within its empire, it leaves little room for concerns with wars outside of it."

"Wars?"

"Yes, it was three years ago. A war with the Prussians and the Germans. My father was like your uncle: a merchant, but a very rich one. He made glass, and mirrors. He was afraid that the war would cause him to lose everything, that I would be alone, unprotected. He asked friends of his, who were coming here, to take me with them. He gave those friends a great deal of money, to serve as my dowry."

Lady Grey fell silent. Rose allowed the silence to last as long as she could. "Lady Grey, forgive me, but... your father... did he..."

Lady Grey smiled sadly. "He was very lucky. He did not die, and he did not lose all he had. At the end of the conflict, my hometown was in German territory. Everyone was given a choice: they could become German and stay, or remain French and leave. My father chose to stay. He is now called Martin Spiegleman, and I am Charlotte Grey. We are no longer French, neither of us. We correspond. It is not easy, being so far away from him, and having so little contact, but what little I have comforts me. It could have been so much worse."

"Do you have no other family, Lady Grey?"

"None I have any contact with. My mother died when I was still in school. My younger brother, when the conflict ended, he chose to remain French and he left for Paris, with nothing but the clothes on his back. I can only hope he manages to get by. He was a clever boy, he might even have done well for himself. But we do not know each other's addresses; we have no way of communicating. I have uncles and aunts and cousins, but no one I ever felt truly close to."

The discussion was getting very difficult for Rose. She was certain that the young Lady Grey would be horrified to receive any pity from her, and yet she could not help herself. She could only imagine what the other woman felt, fleeing her country under the threat of war, and separated from everything and everyone she knew.

She tried to change the subject. "Perhaps your father will come to visit, to meet his grandchild. How did he take the news?"

"I do not know. I only sent him the letter this week. I wanted to be sure. You see... you must have wondered, that this was my first child; a young, healthy couple, married for three years now."

"I had not, milady." That much was the truth. Rose knew precious little of those marital affairs.

Many couples, including her own parents, God rest their souls, had children so fast that one could wonder if they had been conceived out of wedlock. Others could take a year or two, or many more, or, in the case of her aunt and uncle, have no children at all. It seemed a great mystery to her.

"That would be quite the novelty. In any way, I have been pregnant before. But... well... the doctors have told me many things. There were all sorts of instructions this time. I hope for the best."

Rose could think of nothing to say. She took Lady Grey's hand, hoping to convey what little comfort she could offer. The two women sat in silence until the gentlemen returned to the room.

"Very well, then," announced the baron as he walked in. "The card table will be brought out shortly. Until it arrives, I recommend a song to pass the time."

"Oh yes, my lord!" The viscountess could barely contain her excitement at the opportunity to let her protégé shine. "You must allow Miss Fraser to do the honors. I do declare that she is the most accomplished musician I have ever heard, and it is not praise I give lightly. You are in for a treat, sir."

The baron smiled indulgently at his friend. "With this kind of praise, how can I resist? Miss Fraser, if you would do us the honor."

Lady Grey and Rose both got to their feet at the same time, the former guiding the latter to the piano. As Rose took her seat, Lady Grey fetched some sheet music. Rose guessed, or at least hoped, that the future baroness was choosing a piece that the current baron especially liked.

A part of her hoped that the piece in question would be challenging enough to showcase her skill. But on the other hand, as she had not spent nearly enough time practicing in the last month, perhaps a simpler piece would be better. She was glad to have the choice taken out of her hands.

Rose almost sighed in relief when she saw the chosen piece: it was one she knew very well. Her voice was not as strong as her fingers were, but it was nonetheless pleasant, and the joy she found in the music charmed the company. Her mastery of the instrument was a source of amazement for Lady Grey, who could not help but exclaim over the applause: "My God, Miss Fraser, that was astonishing! You played with your eyes closed."

The comment left Rose mortified; would her host think her a braggart? Lady Grey blushed at the embarrassment she caused her guest. "Pray forgive me, Miss Fraser, I did not mean..."

"Think nothing of it, Lady Grey. You only spoke the truth, after all: I was playing with my eyes closed." Rose felt no anger toward Lady Grey, only toward herself, that she allowed herself to be carried away thusly. Her aunt had warned her many times that she spent too much time at the piano. She should have listened.

Lord Albert, taking no notice of the ladies' embarrassment, laughed out loud in delight, and quickly demanded that Rose play another song from memory, and another, and another, until her throat felt sore and Mr. Grey castigated his brother, "For God's sake, Albert, she's not an automaton."

Lady Grey murmured apologies for unwittingly making Rose a victim of her husband's strange sense of humor. The baron ordered a glass of water fetched for her and made small talk with her at the card table until she was certain that she had not made a bragging fool of herself after all.

But it was Mr. Grey who made the incident, and, in fact, the whole evening worthwhile, when he slipped behind her as the two card tables were set, and whispered into her ear: "You were wonderful."

***

After several hands of cards, the evening drew to an end. A carriage was called for the Edwards and Miss Fraser, and the Grey family courteously saw them off, before joining the viscountess back in the drawing room.

"Well, my lord," she asked the baron. "Was my protégé not everything I promised she would be?"

"She was all that and more, milady. I would wish her better relatives, though. What of her parents?"

"They died many years ago. Her mother was the sister of Mr. Edwards, and her father was the second son of the Viscount Southam."

"The second son? I remember something of him. A bit of a rogue, if I recall correctly, though the family had yet to turn their backs on him. Her lineage will do, but it leaves the problem of her guardians. The uncle was passable, in short doses, but the aunt..."

It was obvious in the baron's tone of voice that entertaining Mrs. Edwards was not something he had enjoyed or looked forward to in the future, and the present company agreed with him.

"It may not be quite so bad," spoke Albert. "Mr. Edwards seemed eager to return to the North, and I can't imagine that they'll return much to town, after they leave."

"I wouldn't be too sure of that, my son. She appeared to be of the sort. Once these people have had a taste of higher society, they always come back for more."

"We can always give her the cold shoulder after the wedding. An unpleasant aunt is no reason to turn such a lovely, talented young lady away from the family. How long do you think it would take her to learn a new song?"

"You've yet to find a song she could not play from memory," said James.

"I was interrupted."

"Perhaps it is time for us to go home, my dear," softly spoke Lady Grey. "You may have had too much brandy again."

"I did no such thing. Didn't you like James' little piano player?"

"I did, which is why, should I see her again, I would do my best not to embarrass her."

While Lord Albert Grey protested at his wife's accusation, the viscountess offered to take them both home in her carriage. Soon James was left alone with his father.

"I suppose you'll be speaking with the uncle soon," said the baron.

"That is my intention," answered James. "However, there is one small matter I must take care of first."

The baron found his son's words suspicious. "And what is that?"

"You see, father," James took his time answering. He wanted to present the problem in the best possible light, the one least likely to upset his father. He was forced to admit that such a feat was beyond his capability. "The carriage accident, involving Albert, Miss Fraser and her uncle? I believe it was not an accident."

"James..."

"Miss Fraser has been receiving anonymous threats since she first arrived to town. She shared those threats with me, and I volunteered to discover the identity of her tormentor."

"Damnation, James! You just can't help yourself, can you? Every single time... I have half a mind to forbid you to see the girl at all."

"It would do no good, father," James's tone reflected his reaction to his father's threat: darker and only more determined. "I have given my word to Miss Fraser, and beyond that, I care for her, too much to let her deal with this situation alone. I am of age, and my intentions are honorable. Your consent would be desirable, but it is in no way necessary."

The baron grumbled for a moment longer. "Why not marry her right away, then?" he finally asked. "Take her under your protection, and keep her away from harm?"

"With the bans running for three weeks prior to the ceremony, the news of the wedding would have time to spread far and wide. From the nature of the threats against Miss Fraser, I have reasons to believe that her tormentor would be angered by our engagement, and would attempt to hurt her, and possibly me as well."

The baron took in deep breath, paced a little, and took some time to think the problem through. "How close are you to discovering the identity of this man?"

"I have a few ideas."

"You have one month. I will call in a few favors, obtain a special license for you. If you have not discovered the tormentor by then, you will turn the matter over to someone else. If you do find him... I beg of you, James, please, do not pursue him yourself. Go to the police."

Chapter 9

James left his horse at the nearest stable, and made his way to the corner of Golden Green Road and Finchley Road on foot. When he had sent Will to pursue this particular investigative avenue, he had not expected such a swift response. It might be a wild goose chase, but there was always a chance that this hour long trip would result in good information.

He found his informant leaning against a wall, smoking a cigarette.

"Hello, Will. So, where to?"

Will exhaled his smoke, pointing to a building a few blocks away. "Over there. You know, I looked pretty stupid, asking around about paper."

"Will, as much as I care about you, which, to be perfectly frank, isn't that much at all, your reputation is the least of my concerns."

"Fair enough. Lots of people here are into paper folding. Apparently, it's a thing, where they're from. They make animals, mostly. Not what you asked for, but you know, folding paper is folding paper, right? Anyway, that guy's supposed to be special. Gives lessons, too."

"Well done, boy." James gave Will a small pouch, holding the amount of money previously agreed upon. "I will see what I can make out of this."

Will offered a quick, sarcastic salute and turned away as James walked up to the building where the paper folding teacher would be found. Inside was a small man, hunched over a table, folding a bird of some sort out of colorful paper. Garlands of flowers hung from the wall. James was surprised that their perfume was not more powerful.

"Hum, hello?"

The little man looked up as James called out to him. He lifted the paper bird he had created. "Tsuru," he said. "A crane. In my culture, it is a holy beast, a symbol of honor and loyalty. The legend says that one who folds a Shenbazuru, a string of one thousand cranes, gets one wish in return."

The man pointed to what James had believed to be flowers, but now recognized to be thousands of paper birds strung together.

"You have had many wishes granted, then."

"I have health and good fortune, I need no more. These are for sale. They are popular gifts for weddings, or the birth of a child. One happy year for every crane. How can I help you, sir?"

"I've heard that you teach how to make those paper cranes. Is that true?"

"Yes. I teach origami, and the crane is one of the forms my students wish to learn. It is a popular one."

"What about this form? Is it popular?" James held up a sheet of paper he had folded, following the pattern of the threats Miss Fraser had received.

"Ah..." said the master as he took the folded paper. "What a clever design. It is not one I teach, in fact, I do not believe I have ever seen it before."

"So no one you know teaches it, then?"

"I fear not. When a person comes to me to learn origami, especially when that person is British, they wish to learn a party trick. Something to impress other people. This design is too prosaic. Why do you ask?"

"I am looking for someone who sends anonymous messages, delivered in this folded shape."

"I wish I could be of more help to you. Here," the little man took the crane he had been working on and handed it over to James. "Honor and loyalty to you, and perhaps a bit of luck, as well."

***

Louisa Edwards was a very difficult woman, hard to please, and easy to provoke. The success of her ward with such a family as the Greys of Rotherfield would have satisfied anyone else. Not her. She felt that her niece was too hasty, and too obvious too, in making a choice of a husband. Rose liked the boy, very well, but she should have known better than to show it as she did, seeking him out in public, charming his family. Any other potential husband was already keeping a careful distance, which was why only he paid any attention to her. The chit was so blindly devoted that Mrs. Edwards expected an elopement to Gretna Green at any moment. She suspected that she was not the only one, as well. People were probably already looking through the papers for the announcement. If any kind of proper wedding was to be had, it would need to happen soon. Otherwise, they would be forced into a humiliating elopement, or an exile back to the North. The season was ruined.

Mrs. Edwards was still fuming over the lost possibilities when she saw that Robinson was making his way toward Rose, holding a piece of paper. This only served to further her anger. The mystery that was those notes irritated her. For as long as the family had been in town, they had been arriving, and Rose had never said a word about them. It must have been a dangerous scandal her niece was brewing, or she would not have been keeping it a secret. It would not surprise Mrs. Edwards at all if the ignorant girl were to ruin herself in some scandalous affair. Blood speaks.

"Robinson! I will take this note."

Robinson, respectful of law and propriety as he was, would never have given a missive to anyone other than its designated receiver. However, he hesitated a moment as his mistress called out to him, and that moment was all Aunt Edwards needed to make her way to him and grab the note.

Rose observed her aunt warily as she opened and read the latest message from her tormentor. Her nerves grew as she watched her aunt's face take a truly terrifying expression, with her lips pinched, her nostrils flaring and her eyes bulging.

Mrs. Edwards tore the note and threw the pieces in the fireplace.

"You listen to me, Robinson, and you listen well. None of those filthy notes are ever to cross the threshold of this house again, do you hear me? I do not permit it. If I see you or any other servant carrying one, whoever it is will be laid off and thrown out of the house!"

Aunt Edwards then turned to face Rose.

"What have you done?"

"My aunt?"

"Do you think I will tolerate this type of behavior? Here, and now, after all this time? After all this work? I should have thrown you out on the streets fifteen years ago. I knew you would turn out badly, I have always known. Now you have ruined yourself, and humiliated me, in front of all the town!"

"But, my aunt..." Rose nervously got up on her feet.

"Be quiet, you little trollop!"

On those words, Aunt Edwards pushed Rose, who fell back into her chair.

"Madam!"

A scandalized Robinson rushed to the side of his mistress, while Rose fled from the room as fast as she could. She ran blindly through the house, running up stairs when she found them, turning away when she heard footsteps or voices, until she reached the least visited part of the house: the attic.

Once she was safely alone, behind the closed door, only then did she let the tears flow from her eyes. It was what she had feared all along: that the writings of her tormentor, if brought to light, would cause her to be universally reviled. Her own aunt, the only mother she remembered, had turned against her because of this man.

Mr. Grey had not been repulsed by the notes, but she did not dare to hope that his family would react in a similar manner. The idea that they would still accept her, despite the scandal that would make her own blood reject her, felt impossible.

The only hope for a future with Mr. Grey, therefore, rested in his willingness to elope with her. Rose could not help but hope that he would, and she despised herself for it. She knew she should not wish this kind of choice, this kind of misery, on anyone, and yet she did. The idea of losing Mr. Grey due to the machinations of this man made her heart stop.

After several minutes of struggle, Rose managed to get her emotions under control. Her aunt was furious at the moment, but cooler heads would prevail, surely. The contents of the note, whatever they had been, were not public knowledge. Aunt Edwards would not wish to leave the great London society until she was forced to. It would give Rose some time to find Mr. Grey and discuss the matter with him. He might have a solution, and even if he did not, he would know what to say.

As she wiped the final stray tears from her face, Rose took a moment to observe her surroundings. She had never been in the attic before. It was filled with all manners of strange objects, all of which belonged to previous residents of the house: out of style clothes and cookware, including a giant iron pot; many old pieces of furniture, many covered in broken or useless knick-knacks.

Rose was surprised to find a perfectly good square of flint abandoned on an old dresser. People had been using matches for many years, but there were terrible side effects to the toxic fumes they emitted. Flint was much safer to use, and just as reliable.

Before she could further ponder on why the previous owner would leave behind this particular object, she heard three knocks on the door.

"Rose?" Uncle Edwards asked. "Are you in there?"

Rose dropped the flint back on the dresser. "Yes, Uncle."

She turned around as her uncle opened the attic door. "I've spoken with your aunt."

Rose's heart rose to her throat; she could say nothing.

"Or, should I say, I tried to; she was in hysterics when I came home. Robinson told me that this was about some note, and that her reaction was very strong, and had upset you. I can see that he was right, about the last part at least."

Rose rubbed her hand over her dried cheek, as if the marks of her crying spell could be so easily erased.

"I am sorry that this happened to you, and I can promise you that it will not happen again. Do you feel well enough to come to dinner? I can arrange to have a tray sent up to you."

"Thank you, uncle, but that won't be necessary. I feel well enough to come to dinner."

"Very well. You might want to run some cold water over your face."

On those words, her uncle turned and left.

This was the first dinner home in a long time. When she arrived in the sitting room, Rose was informed by her aunt that they had sent their apologies. Rose did not know if the change of plans was due to her own supposed ruin, or to the angry red mark on her aunt's cheek. Her aunt did not speak a word through dinner. Whenever she attempted to, Uncle Edwards would loudly clear his throat, and she would fall silent once more.

Things were changing, and Rose could not tell if it was for good or for ill.

***

While her aunt's lashing out, followed by her cold shoulder, were troubling to Rose, she still felt slightly better the next day. Her aunt had forbidden any more notes to enter the house. She had no doubt that the man would find some other way to reach her, but surely this would give her some peace, if only for a little while.

Unfortunately, she was wrong. The next evening, she retired to her room after an exhausting dinner party to find a terrifyingly familiar looking folded piece of paper, left on her vanity table.

The note was longer than any of the previous ones had been.

You must understand, Miss Fraser,

That yesterday's events, though unfortunate,

Were unavoidable

This city is ruining you

Just as it ruined your mother

If you remain, you will lose everyone

You will lose everything

Even your life

Just as she did

***

"The note was left in your room?" asked Mr. Grey the following night. They had both been invited to the same ball, and he asked her for the longest waltz, as well as the following dance. The precaution had proven useful, for Aunt Edwards was watching her closer than ever before, and they had much to talk about.

Rose answered Mr. Grey's question with a nod. "He must live with us. It is the only way, isn't it? How else could he get to my room?"

"There are a few other ways. He could have befriended one of your domestics. He used street boys to deliver the first messages, he could have hired a thief to deliver this one. Someone who makes a specialty of entering other people's houses."

Rose shuddered at these words.

"I did not mean to frighten you, Miss Fraser," Mr. Grey quickly added. "It was merely a theory."

"I don't believe you could help frightening me, Mr. Grey. Everything about this situation is frightening. I can't decide which would be worse: if this man was a complete stranger or someone I know. Sir, do you think that man killed my parents?"

Mr. Grey appeared surprised by her question. "No, I must admit that this possibility eluded me. What made you ask?"

"It was just... the way he spoke of my mother, in this note. That her death was unavoidable, that she was ruined. It wasn't true, none of it. But maybe to him..."

"Maybe. It is just as likely, however, that the man writing these notes has researched you and your family's history, and that he chose the words that would upset you the most. Perhaps it is retaliation for letting your aunt read the note."

"But I had no control over that."

"You are in a position to be punished, though, and for this type of person, it is enough."

Rose could not decide whether this new possibility was less frightening than the previous one. "Pray, sir, tell me you found something."

"I believe I did. I am pursuing an investigative avenue which sounds extremely promising." He proceeded to tell her about his visit to an oriental man who worked outside of town, teaching others the art of folding paper.

"I do not understand," she finally said. "How was that visit helpful? Do you think the man was lying?"

"No, I don't. I believe he was telling the truth when he said he never saw the design, which makes me think that our villain created it himself. This would mean that he has been studying origami for quite some time. You told me yourself that from the day of the viscountess's invitation to your arrival in town, only a fortnight had passed. This would not be nearly enough time. I therefore believe that the man we are looking for followed you from the North, where he has studied at a different school of paper folding."

"Or perhaps he is a Londoner who studied a long time ago. Someone who knew my parents." The idea that her tormentor was also her parents' killer was solidly anchored in Rose's mind, and would not easily leave, despite Mr. Grey's reassurances.

"That is also a possibility. I shall research your parents' history, see what I can find of their circle of acquaintances. I will leave no stone unturned, Miss Fraser. You can count on me."

"I know, Mr. Grey. I trust you."

***

James spent the following week keeping his promise to Miss Fraser. He looked into her parents' past, tried to find some friends and acquaintances. The task was more challenging than he had expected. From what his father had said of the departed Alexander Fraser, Esquire, he figured there would be several mentions in the society pages. But the couple apparently led a quiet, almost sheltered life.

It appeared that marriage did a world of good to the youngest son of Viscount Southam. Prior to the happy event, his name had appeared in many betting books, and in the society pages. Mr. Fraser had been, to put it simply, a rake and a rogue.

There were no bans for the wedding of Alexander Fraser and Florence Edwards. Merely an announcement, which was, in and of itself, unusual. The wedding was followed, some ten months afterward, by the birth of Miss Fraser. Late enough that no one won the betting pools of the gentlemen's club, but still soon enough to allow some innuendo, from what James could read.

After the birth of Miss Fraser, her parents remained out of the public eye, until they were murdered. The news articles of the time reported that a burglar broke in and accidentally woke the Frasers. The thief stabbed first Mr. Fraser, and then Mrs. Fraser. Mrs. Fraser's scream had alerted the servants, and the thief ran away. No good descriptions could be given of the man, nor any consistent account of missing items.

James was inclined to agree with Miss Fraser that there might be something more to this crime than it appeared. Thieves and murderers were two different kinds of people. A man who made a living breaking into people's houses would be more likely to avoid the residents, and he would not unnecessarily burden himself with a weapon.

That being said, he could find no motive for a killing, not during their married life. It was possible that Mr. Fraser had made a few enemies prior to his union with

Mrs. Fraser, but an offense which would justify a murder three years after the fact seemed unlikely to him.

Unless the intended victim was Mrs. Fraser, the former Miss Edwards. The wedding and birth announcements were only published in London papers. Someone looking for her, from the North, would have needed more time to find her than it would have taken a native Londoner to find the son of a viscount.

However, his study of Mrs. Fraser's past gave very little in the way of leads. He found the marriage announcements of Miss Fraser's grandparents, Harold and Frances Edwards. He found her birth announcement of twins Florence and George, Miss Fraser's mother and her uncle.

He found the wedding announcement of Mr. George Edwards to Miss Louisa Smith. Miss Smith, five-and-twenty years of age at the time of the wedding, seemed an odd choice for a bride. Far past her prime, and not very attractive to say the least, she brought nothing more to the wedding than a few abandoned buildings. Harold Edwards turned these buildings into factories, and launched his business. Perhaps that had been his goal all along.

He found that Mr. George Edwards joined the army and fought in the Pacific during the Crimean war. Miss Edwards met and married Mr. Fraser while her brother was at the front. He was injured at Petropavlovsk and discharged in 1855. The timing was fortuitous, for around the same time, his father was killed in a hunting accident. Mrs. Harold Edwards died a few days later in her sleep. Mr. Edwards took over the business of his father. After the death of his sister, he went to London and returned with a very young Miss Fraser, who now his ward.

Such was the sum total of Mrs. Fraser's history, and he could hardly find a motive for murder in it. He could only think of two: a disgruntled business partner trying to get more control over the company by threatening, and eventually killing, family members, or a former paramour, driven mad by her marriage. As he could hardly imagine that either motive would justify the threats against Miss Fraser now, fifteen years later, he would have no problems telling her that whatever happened to her parents and her current dilemma were unrelated.

Still... it did make for a rather troubling coincidence. And if a rather suspicious someone were to add the death of Harold Edwards... A hunting accident could cover many things.

Perhaps it would be better to send someone up North, to dig a little deeper. For the sake of absolute certainty.

Chapter 10

Time stopped for no man, and neither did the season. As the temperature in town became ever more difficult to bear, several of the better families retired to their country estate, which gave them the perfect opportunity to throw large parties. In this, as in every other thing, the peers competed with each other: it became a matter of who had the best estate, the most exclusive guest list, the most entertaining activities.

Seaside estates had gained popularity over the last few years, and it was a wonderful accident of fate that Lord Harris, one of Albert Grey's close friends, had access to such an estate near Westgate-on-Sea and was planning a getaway. The party would include close to fifty people, and last a month, if the rumors were to be believed.

It went without saying that Lord and Lady Albert Grey were on the prestigious guest list. Eager as they were to further their acquaintance with Miss Fraser, and to ensure that she would soon be a part of the family, they procured invitations for her and James. They also paid a call to Mrs. Edwards, to convince her that Charlotte would be an adequate chaperon.

Both Lord and Lady Grey expected the second of those errands to be the most difficult. There was something

117

almost frightening about the ease with which Mrs. Edwards handed over her ward to them.

"If you want the chit, you are more than welcome. I am well rid of her."

"What would possess her to say such a thing?" Lady Grey asked her husband after they had departed from Mrs. Edwards's company.

"She's an unpleasant woman, unpleasant things must be expected of her," was his answer.

"I suppose. But it seemed awfully peculiar."

"Never you mind, my dear. We have obtained what we were hoping for; James's little piano prodigy will come with us to the seaside. Mrs. Edwards's loss is our gain, and I say that's the end of the matter."

Lady Grey could think of no reason to argue further with her husband, and thus the discussion ended. They therefore went to find James and tell him the good news.

In the Edwards household, the news only brought more tension. Uncle Edwards was unhappy that his wife would so readily abdicate her duties as a chaperon, to which Aunt Edwards used the careful though accurate excuse that one does not refuse a request from a future baron.

Early in the morning of the day before the departure for the seaside estate, Uncle Edwards received a telegram from the man he had left in charge of his business. His presence was required in the North, urgently.

He left within the hour.

Aunt Edwards then dragged Rose out for their customary walk in the park, more out of boredom then out of any desire to be seen out in public with her niece. She came to regret the impulse; they had not been in a park ten minutes when they crossed paths with Lord and Lady Grey, who were accompanied by Mr. James Grey.

James, his brother, and his sister-in-law ignored Mrs. Edwards as much as their manners would allow them to, and turned their attention to Miss Fraser. James was especially interested to learn that Mr. Edwards had left town. He had been toying with the idea of asking the man a few questions about Miss Fraser's parents. Mr. Edwards's attitude toward James had been cold, that much was true, but then again, his attitude in general seemed standoffish. Miss Fraser had confessed to him that her uncle had been opposed to their coming to London. Perhaps he was uncomfortable here. Perhaps, in his hometown, he would be more likely to open up.

James had already made up his mind to send Will up North to look for an origami school up there. It would be little trouble for the boy to track Mr. Edwards and ask him a few questions. Of course, Will would have to prove that he could blend in the better world. Perhaps James should send someone else with him, to do the talking.

***

Rose was sitting in the train cabin the Greys had obtained, travelling west toward Kent and Westage-on-Sea. She was sitting next to Lady Grey. Mr. Grey and his brother Lord Grey sat in front of them. As they left the city and made their way toward the seaside estate of Lord Grey's friend, she tried to loosen the great weight she felt on her shoulders. She was away from her aunt's judgment, away from her uncle's mercurial moods, and most importantly, away from her tormentor.

This was not the time to think about the notes that continually appeared on her vanity table, every new note a reference to her mother's supposedly depraved life and death. This was a time to get to know the Grey family better. She was immensely grateful that Lord and Lady Grey had extended this invitation to her, and she was determined to be the best possible guest to them. She would remain of a good humor, no matter what.

She had many things to distract herself from her worries, after all. It was the first time she had gone anywhere on a train. She found her opinion of the mode of transportation much different than that of her aunt. It was loud, yes, but it was very clean, from what she could see, and there were many, many people taking the train, making it obvious that it was fit for passengers as well as cargo.

If the experience of train travel was not distracting enough to take her mind off her worries, the stories told by her companions certainly were. They told her tales of the people she could expect to meet, and of the town she was about to visit. There were far too many names and far too much information for her to remember anything about the guests, but the story of Westgate-on-Sea was fascinating. Twelve years ago, the land which was now a vacation spot had been farmland. Investors started buying plots of land about a decade ago, and among those investors had been Lord Harris's father.

"Such as in Sanditon, by Miss Jane Austen?" asked Rose.

"In a manner of speaking, yes," answered Lady Grey, while Mr. Grey and Lord Grey looked confused.

She was entertained, without a doubt. But still, whenever someone walked in front of their cabin, she could not help but jump, and would need several minutes afterward to convince herself that her tormentor was not on the train, that Mr. Grey and his family were right there with her, and that she was safe.

***

Westgate-on-Sea really started to grow when the train had reached the town the previous year. As they arrived to their destination, Mr. Grey pointed out the steeple of the church currently being built. From the train station, they took a carriage to Lord Harris's estate. Rose did her best not to look out the window at the road behind them. Such an action was unnecessary; no one was following them.

The journey went without a hitch, and they soon found themselves on a beautiful property, with what may have been the biggest house Rose had ever seen, and a view of the ocean that took her breath away.

The flow of newly arriving guests was steady, and the rounds of introductions seemed never ending. Rose felt intimidated by such a crowd, but she was pleased that many seemed to be close to her age. Her aunt had preferred the society of matrons to that of the newly married and the debutantes.

Though the guests were mainly Lord Grey's friends, Mr. Grey could boast of a few connections of his own in the party. He introduced Rose to a Mr. Cowper, a friend of his who proceeded to regale them with his tale of woes. He was attempting to court a certain Lady Newport, but fate conspired against him, throwing him at a certain Lady Dunwich at every turn. Neither lady was present at the outing, which Rose understood was a blessing of sorts, as Lady Newport was very fond of Lady Dunwich, and criticizing her friend would end the possibility of the courtship as quickly as marrying said friend. Mr. Grey teased Mr. Cowper: was he thinking of marrying lady Dunwich, then? Mr. Cowper had no answer, which amused Mr. Grey even more.

She answered queries about herself, and made small talk when required. But otherwise, she spoke little, preferring to watch the guests arrive and listen to the reactions of the rest of the party. She tried not to shiver when a male guest would comment on having noticed her at such-and-such, or ask a specific question about her activities, or about her family. She told herself that most guests were too young to have known her parents. Most.

One guest caused a particularly strong reaction among the other guests. Lady Grey herself turned to her husband and asked, "Why did you not tell me he was coming," to which he answered, "I didn't know. The news doesn't please me either, but let us look at the bright side. This is a big estate, it shouldn't be too hard to avoid him."

"I'm sorry, my Lord, my Lady," interrupted Rose. "Who is this man you speak of?"

"His name, not that you'll ever need to use it, is Mr. Forrest," answered Lady Grey. "He is a reprobate, there are no other words. He married the daughter of a newspaper owner, by some sort of blackmail, apparently, and forced his father-in-law to employ him as a journalist. He uses this supposed profession as an excuse to freely move about with criminals and women of little virtue."

"He also attends many high society events, sometimes through the connections of his father-in-law, sometimes because the host is courting some scandal," continued Lord Grey. "And on the subject of the latter, he never disappoints. He says the most offensive things, he cheats at cards, he even brings his little playthings, as if they had any right to parade themselves among their betters."

"But," Rose said, "if his father-in-law is employing him, surely he won't tolerate the spectacle he makes, flaunting other women when his daughter is sure to hear of it."

"And yet he does," answered Mr. Grey, "which is why the consensus is that the marriage was somehow forced, by the groom, who wanted the connection for some reason. Conveniently enough, Mrs. Forrest is apparently of a nervous disposition, and spends most of her time bedridden, while her husband is out on the town."

As Mr. Grey finished his explanation, Lady Grey turned to Mr. Forrest's carriage once more. "Oh dear me!" she exclaimed, turning away sharply. "He brought one of them, here. Some redheaded tart."

"We can avoid them, my dear," Lord Grey reminded his wife as he held a comforting arm around her.

Rose could not resist looking in the direction previously indicated by Lady Grey. She soon regretted the impulse. She recognized the woman Lady Grey just described as a tart, the only woman standing in that direction who had red hair, currently pressed indecently against a slightly older, somewhat attractive man.

Her former friend Mary Jones.

***

Things were not going as well as James had expected. It could be worse, certainly it could be much worse, but it could also be better.

Miss Fraser had confessed her former acquaintance with Mr. Forrest's companion, Miss Jones. She was quick to explain that there were very few girls her own age in her neighborhood. That the two girls had lost touch over the years, since Mr. Jones had been elected to the House of Commons and moved the family to London. That she noticed in London how much Miss Jones had changed, and that she had already resolved not to speak with her anymore.

She seemed so nervous at the idea that the Greys would think less of her, as if such a thing was possible.

Quite the opposite, in fact: they thanked her for the trust she showed them, and endeavored to do everything in their power to assure that Miss Fraser would never have to spend a moment alone in the company of either Mr. Forrest or Miss Jones.

Which was much easier said than done, considering the fact that Miss Jones was seeking out the company of Miss Fraser very persistently, and was quite obtuse in her refusal to see that her presence was not desired by any means. As Miss Fraser, sensitive and delicate as she was, found it difficult to openly snob a former friend, the Greys made a point of honor to never leave her unattended. They even arranged for Bernadette, the maid Lady Harris had provided for Miss Fraser, to remain at her side whenever the Greys had to leave her alone. This could have been avoided if Mrs Edwards had allowed Miss Fraser's maid to accompany them, but Mrs Edwards had been in a particular mood these past few days.

James had hoped that the holiday would be beneficial to Miss Fraser. That with a change of scenery, far away from her troubles in the city, and some time away from her judgmental aunt and her passive uncle, she would be able to take pleasure in the activities of the season, to truly enjoy herself.

Instead, he watched from across the room as she sat, her posture tense and her eyes sad. The entertainment provided by their hosts that night consisted of various oriental puzzles, with the alleged ability to drive lesser men out of their feeble minds.

He was paying more attention to Miss Fraser then to the hosts passing the games around. He noticed right away that a servant was making his way toward her, holding a seemingly empty dish, the kind used to carry around letters. But he was completely taken by surprise when a man stepped in front of him, holding one of the toys out to him.

"Come now, Grey. Let's see if you are as clever as you think you are."

With the annoying little man blocking his path, James could do nothing but watch as the servant presented the dish to Miss Fraser. She blanched and picked up the note with a trembling hand.

A small crowd had gathered around him, looking at his hands expectantly. A few men, rowdier than the rest, started to jeer him, mocking his supposed cowardice. There was no way for James to make his way to Miss Fraser without causing a scene. He had to solve the silly puzzle first, or at least try.

He therefore turned his attention to the problem at hand. The obvious goal here was to push some small ball out of a vertical labyrinth, using a thin wooden shaft. James solved the puzzle in a little over two minutes.

"Excuse me," he said, giving the toy back to his host before walking away.

The man was flabbergasted. "How did he do it so fast?" James heard him ask behind his back. James allowed himself a small smile as he continued without pause. Even in the hypothetical case where he didn't have more pressing matters at the moment, he would have kept the truth to himself. The polite society would only be confused, if not shocked, that the youngest son of a baron would spend the last six months training himself in the art of lock-picking.

After a quick detour, James walked up to Miss Fraser, a glass of iced tea in his hands. She kept her eyes closed, her weariness obvious.

"Miss Fraser, you seem unwell. May I offer you a refreshment?"

Her words of thanks were barely audible as she took the glass. He in turn took the note from her, in a gesture he hoped had been subtle. He did not notice anyone looking at him suspiciously, aside from his sister-in-law. He would have to explain to her, and to his brother as well, when they were alone.

Miss Fraser had not touched the iced tea. She remained unmoving, defeated.

"Perhaps you should rest," said Charlotte. "I'll escort you upstairs." She took Miss Fraser by the arm.

Together, they slowly made their way out of the room.

***

Charlotte walked into Miss Fraser's room softly, hoping not to startle her. She found Miss Fraser sitting on the bed, staring out into nothing. Charlotte silently dismissed Bernadette, the maid they put in charge of keeping Miss Fraser company, to discourage Miss Jones from associating with her.

"Miss Fraser?" she called softly. Her young friend turned her head at the sound, and the expression on the poor girl's face was heartbreaking.

"I was hoping a little rest would do you some good."

"I'm sorry, milady," answered Miss Fraser. "I couldn't..."

Miss Fraser didn't finish her sentence, and truly, it was unnecessary for her to do so. Charlotte made her way to the small washbasin, and took the washcloth there. After a quick dab in the cool water, Charlotte handed the cloth to Miss Fraser.

"Here. You should at least freshen up a little."

Miss Fraser took the washcloth and brushed it over her eyes and cheeks a few times. Then she held it against her cheek. Charlotte could not bear to see her so unhappy, so defeated; she attempted to give her some comfort.

"James told us about your situation."

The sentence did not have the desired effect. Indeed, Charlotte felt her own panic rising as Miss Fraser buried her face in the cloth and started to cry.

Charlotte rushed to her and wrapped her in her arms. Among her own 'there, there's', she caught a murmur. Miss Fraser kept repeating 'I'm sorry', over and over again.

"Please, Miss Fraser. You have nothing to apologize for. Calm yourself, I beg you. All will be well."

Miss Fraser looked up to her, her expression incredulous. "But," she said, "You said... but the baron... what about... doesn't he..."

Did the sweet child believe that the Baron would turn her away because of this unfortunate occurrence? Others might, but surely not the baron. He would not reject a perfectly lovely young woman, who was in no way responsible for her current dreadful situation, and who was the best hope he had of seeing his youngest son domesticated.

"Yes, the baron knows. He doesn't think any less of you for this. Why would he?"

"Truly?"

"Yes, truly," insisted Charlotte. "He does believe that James is making his own life exceedingly more difficult then he needs to; we all do. No one doubts that marrying you would keep you safe. But James argues that the three weeks publications of the bans would put you in danger, so the baron is working on obtaining a special license for you. Once you are married, you may take a long honeymoon on the continent while we turn the matter over to the police. Hopefully, James won't let his pride get in the way."

"I... I don't know what to do," Miss Fraser said after a moment. She looked completely lost. "I can't imagine going to the police, with nothing more than a few notes and a carriage accident. Even if I could convince them to take me seriously, my aunt would be so embarrassed, so upset. She read one of the notes, and she was so angry. She has barely spoken a word to me since. If the police came to talk to her... I can't imagine. And my uncle! He was the one driving the carriage. They will assume that he was involved."

This explained Mrs. Edwards's strange reaction when her husband and she delivered Miss Fraser's invitation, thought Charlotte. As for that 'being taken seriously by the police' nonsense, that must have been James's influence. The police would investigate what they told them to investigate, of course. But James could not accept that; he had to do everything himself.

"There, there, Miss Fraser," she said. "Let us not worry about this for now. We will face these issues soon enough. Let us enjoy this vacation."

"Enjoy it? Lady Grey, the man is here! He followed me!"

"What good will that do for him? You are never alone. The house is full of guests and servants. I have already given instructions to the majordomo: any notes or letters addressed to you with no signature, no return address and no seal are to be destroyed."

"Did Mr. Grey agree to that? I thought he needed these, as evidence."

"My husband and I convinced him that whatever evidence those notes might contain is not worth the distress they cause you. My husband is, at the moment, surveying the guest list. Most of the guests are his friends; he would notice any unusual names. James is at the local inn, doing the same with their registrar. So, you see? The matter is as good as resolved. All you have to do now is calm down, and let Bernadette help you get ready for dinner."

"Yes, Lady Grey."

"Oh, and one more thing: you must call me Charlotte, and I shall call you Rose in return. I must insist, we will soon be sisters, after all."

The smile Charlotte received in return for those words was blinding in its brilliance. "Thank you," said Rose in a soft voice.

Charlotte tapped her cheek affectionately, before rising and calling Bernadette back to the room. She could not be more pleased with a future sister, and she intended to visit on her quite often in the future. Someone would have to keep the dramatic tendencies of the future Mr. and Mrs. James Grey in check.

***

Rose followed as Bernadette lead the way to the dining room. The corridor was unfamiliar, but that did not surprise her; she had only been in the house for a few days after all, and had stuck to the paths between her room and the common areas. She was running a bit late for dinner, and Bernadette suggested that they take the servants' staircase, which was closer.

What surprised and even upset her was how quiet the corridor was.

"Bernadette, where is everyone?"

"Beg your pardon, miss?"

"I can't hear anyone else. I would assume that other servants use this corridor as well, so where are they?"

"Oh, you know. Some in the kitchen or the dining room, some in the rooms upstairs. This spot is usually pretty quiet right about now, that's normal."

Bernadette's words made sense, but the maid was obviously nervous about something, and this only exacerbated Rose's feeling of unease.

A floorboard creaked, somewhere down the corridor. Rose turned toward the noise instinctively, but there was no one out there.

"Did you hear that?" asked Rose sharply.

"I... I don't know, miss."

The sound came again, louder this time. It was moving closer. Rose felt her breath hitch as she peered in the shadows, trying to make out the silhouette. She eased herself backwards, edging herself away from the source of the noise. She tried to get her fear back under control, and was preparing to call out to whoever was out there, when she heard her name, in a slow, rumbling whisper.

"Rose."

She ran.

She turned and ran blindly down the corridor. All she could think of was to get away, as fast as her cumbersome dinner gown would allow. She ran until she tripped, just in front of the stairway. She barely managed to grab on the corner of the wall, and therefore landed on her hip rather than on her head. She rolled halfway down the stairs, her grunts of pain covered by Bernadette's screams.

Chapter 11

Despite the recent expansion due to the train reaching the town, Westgate-on-Sea was still a relatively small town. However, even this small town had benefited from the flocks of Londoners who wished to escape the city and play tourist, and who brought with them many doctors who wanted to open up shop in the most desirable location.

Miss Fraser saw a doctor within the hour of her fall. He declared that she suffered from mild shock and a sprain to her leg. He expected a full recovery, and offered to the patient a vial of tonic, should the dizziness get much worse. He also prescribed that she take plenty of rest, and forbade any strenuous activity, such as dancing, or excessive walking.

James was not appeased by the doctor's prognosis. What he had observed at the scene of the accident caused such a torrent of anger and fear and helplessness in him, nothing could calm him. He therefore had no choice but to do what every man does in this type of situation: he took his anger out on someone else.

"Bernadette!" he called out. "Come with me."

The poor maid had been a shaking, stuttering mess all evening, but that made no difference to James. She had guided Miss Fraser into this deserted corridor, and he was certain that it was no coincidence. She knew something. The question was what.

Once he had her in the corridor where Miss Fraser had been injured, James asked her exactly that. "What do you know?"

"Sir?" asked the confused maid.

"I said, what do you know?"

"Sir, I already said..."

"Yes, I know what you've said," James interrupted the stammering maid. "You haven't told the whole story, though, have you? Want to know how I know this? Here."

James dragged Bernadette to the top of the stairs and pointed out a protruding nail, about five inches up from the floor, with a bit of string still tied to it.

"There is another nail, just like this one, across the frame. The string was laid out with the intent to trip someone. But no one was there, except for you and Miss Fraser. You knew that. You knew the corridor would be empty when you lured her here, to a trap, so she could get hurt."

"I didn't know! He said he just wanted to talk to her!"

The maid's teary confession was precisely what James had hoped for.

"Who was he? What was his name?"

"Mr. John Smith." Of course. James barely bit back a sigh at the obvious, but oh so effective ploy, while Bernadette went on. "He said he was a friend of the family, that the Greys didn't approve of him and wouldn't let him talk to her."

That last bit was a surprise, to say the least. "And you believed that?"

"Well, it's like with the red headed woman who's with Mr. Forrest. She's been complaining that she and Miss Fraser used to be friends, but that now, she couldn't get anywhere near her anymore. I didn't know what he planned, I swear. When I realized that he wasn't showing himself, and how scared she was, it was too late to do anything."

It brought great sadness to James that in his attempt to save Miss Fraser some discomfort, he may have given this man an opportunity to harm her. He questioned Bernadette for a while longer, trying to get a better description, some clue that would tell him who the man was. But the maid was not very observant, and she could do no better than "a tall, well-dressed man with gray hair."

The same general description Will had given, which he had in turn given to the manager of the local inn, with no result. James felt he was at an impasse.

***

Rose felt numb. She could not explain the source of this feeling, or lack thereof. Perhaps it was the pain medication prescribed to her. Perhaps it was the effort of dealing with so many people visiting her, keeping them entertained without letting them know how scared and hurt she truly felt. She could not help but think that her tormentor was possibly among the visitors calling on her. She wanted to be left alone, yet she knew that, should she be, he would come back and kill her.

She wished Bernadette was still following her, but as soon as the Greys learned of her implication in the incident, they forbade the maid from approaching Rose. They would not even consider getting another maid to remain at Rose's side; Lady Grey insisted on taking the part herself. She and Lord Albert, who visited as often as propriety would allow, bemoaned the Harris's inability to hire trustworthy servants, and were quick to assure her that such a thing would never have occurred at their house.

Rose was not so sure. She believed that Bernadette had been fooled by this Mr. Smith, and that any servant at any house could have been fooled as well. Still, she did not have the energy to argue with them. She barely had it in her to listen to them, or anyone else, talk. Rose wished only to remain in bed, drink her tonic, and let her mind succumb to the nothingness of sleep. Only Lady Grey's promise that the best orchestra in the county was coming to play for the ball that evening could lure her out of her bedroom. She made her way to the grand ballroom, her mind covered with numbness and her body covered with the most beautiful gown she owned.

The musicians were the best she had ever heard, the food was delicious, and the company, relieved to see her out of her bedchamber and occupied by the current festivities, was very pleasant. Mr. Grey was especially kind and helpful to her. With his kind attentions, and with the support of Lord and Lady Grey, Rose came to enjoy the evening after all.

As the hours passed, the heat in the ballroom became close to unbearable. The French doors were opened, and, as the evening was nice, some guests took the opportunity to walk the grounds, Rose among them.

She was accompanied on her walk by Mr. Grey. In different company, this would have been interpreted as a shocking liberty, a complete want of propriety. But among friends their own age, who understood that a marriage was imminent, it was excused as the impetuousness young lovers ought to show.

They took a turn toward the gardens, Mr. Grey careful to keep a slow pace so Rose would not exert herself. He avoided any subject that might have caused her discomfort, and, rather, discussed what he believed she would judge to be the most pleasant of subjects: the musicians hired for the evening and their art. He agreed with everything she said and paid her every compliment, and she blushed at his words.

This tender moment was interrupted when Mary Jones stepped in front of them, which troubled Rose a great deal. The efforts of the Grey family combined with the most recent events had allowed her to forget Mary's presence at this house for some lengths of time, and she was now feeling not only the anxiety of facing her former friend, but the guilt of having ignored her for so long.

Mr. Grey, on the other hand, looked angrier than she'd ever seen him. He closed his grasp on her more firmly and began to turn around, obviously determined to avoid her.

"Now, wait a minute," exclaimed Mary. "Rose, please, I only want to talk to you."

"A more sensible woman would have realized by now that she's clearly unwanted," answered Mr. Grey.

"I wasn't talking to you, you big bully."

"Don't you think you've done enough damage with your stubborn insolence?"

"Insolence? I'll show you insolence."

Rose was not certain what Mr. Grey meant by "damage", or why he was so angry, but she could tell that the argument would soon escalate, and she felt the need to intervene. "I'll talk to her," she said.

"Miss Fraser, please," Mr. Grey pleaded with her, the idea obviously worrying him a great deal. "You don't have to do this."

"I would prefer to avoid a scene. This will only take a minute." After a few moments, once it became clear that Mr. Grey was determined not to move, she added, "May we have some privacy?"

Mr. Grey composed himself as best he could, bowed slightly to her, and took a few steps away from the two women, turning his back to them. This was as much privacy as could be expected; it would have to do.

"We can no longer be friends."

Mary was visibly upset by Rose's words. "What, because of him? That high society, stiff-necked snob with those archaic rules declares that I'm not good enough, and just like that, a lifetime of friendship gets washed away?"

"Were it only that, it would be enough. I care about those people, Mary. I care about him. I cannot, will not, risk my future with him on the mad gamble that he could be able to accept my friendship with you, in the face of his family and his peers, after what you've become."

"I can't believe this. Don't you see what you're doing to yourself?"

"No, I see what you've done to yourself. After all your talks of independence, you've turned your back on everyone you know and thrown yourself at the mercy of this Mr. Forrest. What will you do when he tires of you, Mary? Have you thought of that? When he decides that you are too common, or too simple, or too old, and he replaces you with some other young, pretty, clever thing, what then? Everyone who knows you will disavow you. I would be shocked if they haven't already. You'll have no one. You'll have nothing but your charms and your wits, which can no doubt be found tenfold elsewhere. You'll die starving on the streets."

"You're wrong," replied Mary. "You've got it all wrong. Forrest isn't in charge of this relationship, I am. He will stay with me as long as it pleases me, and when I tire of him, I'll find another one. I don't need the idiotic, self-important rules of aristocracy. I make my own rules, and live a much better life for it."

The laughter that escaped Rose's lips at this bold declaration was not one of amusement. It was one of bitterness, and exhaustion. "I hope this fantasy gives you what pleasure it may, for as long as it lasts. I must return to reality. Goodbye, Mary."

Rose walked back to Mr. Grey, who, of course, had heard everything. He placed her hand on his arm and guided her back to the ballroom, murmuring soothing reassurances, as she turned her back on her friend for the last time.

***

Sometime later that evening, Mary Jones received a note of her own. There was nothing suspicious or threatening about it, it was merely mysterious. She was to go to a certain room once everyone had retired, and she was to keep the meeting a secret. She could think of no reason not to follow those instructions.

Therefore, an hour or so before dawn, she made her way to the rendezvous point, careful not to be seen. Mary stepped into the room. The curtains were drawn closed, there were no lamps or candles turned on; the room was completely dark.

"Hello? Is anyone there?"

"Close the door."

Mary was a bit shocked at the harshness of the voice, but she did as it asked. There was something familiar about that voice, she was sure that she knew that man. She might not recognize the voice, specifically, but she knew enough to feel confident. She believed that she could handle herself when faced with all of the men among her acquaintances.

"Sit down," the man said once the door was shut.

Mary raised an eyebrow, though of course the man could not see her. He was sure to have heard the impudence in her voice, when she asked: "Where?"

A lamp lit up briefly, from a small table near a chair, before dimming to almost nothing. Mary briefly saw the back of the man, but the light was now so dim, she could hardly make out more than a manly silhouette.

She made her way to the chair. One she was seated, the silhouette walked to the door and locked it. This action made her nervous, but she did what she could not to show it. She was sitting in the light; the man could see her expression even if she couldn't see his.

"You are going to use your influence on Rose. You are going to convince her to end this courtship of hers, with that Grey man."

"Excuse me?"

"This romance of theirs has already gone too far, it's far past time for you to intervene. You've been lounging around, parading with those men and forgetting your duty. That's gone on for long enough. You'll get to work now, or else..."

"Or else what?" Mary said, full of bravado. It was easier to hide her pain at the end of her friendship with Rose if she stayed angry at that man. "I don't know who you are, or who you think you are, but I don't take orders from anyone. I wouldn't do this even if I could; Rose's life is her own, and even if I don't agree with her choices..."

The man interrupted her. "What do you mean, if you could?"

Something about his tone stopped Mary's rant dead in its tracks. It took her a moment to regroup her thoughts. "I mean you're already too late. Rose and I are no longer acquainted. She told me so tonight. She and Mr. Grey were taking a walk along the gardens, unchaperoned. They are as good as married already."

As she spoke, Mary reached for the lamp, to turn it up until she could see the face of the man. She realized her mistake as soon as she recognized the man, and as she took in his expression.

"Well then, Miss Jones, it appears that you have outlived your usefulness."

Chapter 12

The body was discovered very shortly thereafter. Two servants heard the bell ringing in that room, and went to investigate. They were forced to break the door down and found the windows open and the poor woman bleeding from several wounds on her chest. Another similar wound on her back would be revealed upon further examination.

The police was called, and the outraged hosts and guests expected that they would charge the odious Mr. Forrest with the murder of his mistress, because the man was so unpleasant, such a blight on their society. Besides, who else could have done it?

Mr. Forrest was proving most uncooperative in this matter. Not only did he leave no evidence of his presence at the crime scene, but he stubbornly refused to confess. Rather, he wandered around in a state of shock, sometimes raging at the policemen for their vile suggestions, sometimes sobbing until he lost his breath. Everyone was very frustrated with him. They would have been even more frustrated with James, had they known what he thought of the matter: he was inclined to believe Mr. Forrest.

His alibi was far from perfect, as he claimed to have fallen asleep before Miss Jones and had slept like the dead – a poor choice of words, considering the circumstances – until some servant woke him up to inform him that the police wished to speak to him. Nevertheless, there were too many questions which remained unanswered by the simple theory favored by the local police. Evidence indicated that whoever had killed Mary Jones had left the room not through the door, which had been locked from the inside, but through the window. Mr. Forrest's room was on the second floor. How could Mr. Forrest have returned to his room unnoticed? Where was the key to the room? Where was the murder weapon, as a matter of fact?

It felt only natural for him to point out those discrepancies to the constable who had come to deal with the issue. The constable reasonably answered that he had allowed James to look at the crime scene as a courtesy, because he was a friend of the victim's and of her family, but that he didn't like or trust private investigators. Which was why James had lied about being friends with Miss Jones in the first place. It appeared that his clever fiction would only go so far.

As the constable turned back to his suspect, James noticed something on the floor, near the space where the body had been. It was an ivory cameo on a black ribbon. James picked up the pretty piece of jewelry.

"Oi!" said the constable. "What's that?"

"Miss Jones was wearing it last night. It is a family heirloom. Do you see this?" James showed the design of the cameo: a crest bearing three flowers. "This is the Jones family crest. I was hoping you would allow me to return this to Mrs. Jones. It might give her some comfort in the face of this tragedy."

James was, once again, lying. Miss Jones had not worn anything like this around her neck last night. He had no idea if the crest was indeed that of the Jones family. However, he had noticed that, though the area surrounding the body was essentially a pool of blood, the cameo was clean. James suspected that this was no accident, and that the placement of the cameo had been carefully staged. The fact that he had found it with the design facing up only added to this suspicion.

Thankfully, the constable accepted James's explanation, leaving him free to take the cameo and examine it further. What use could this bauble have in a police investigation, after all?

James saw the matter differently. Perhaps it was only a coincidence that it was Miss Fraser's friend that had been murdered, and in that case the cameo would have no investigative value whatsoever. But after the incident in the stairs, and with the notes following them here, it all seemed a little too much for James. He was rather more inclined to believe that this gruesome crime was yet another message to Miss Fraser. In this context, it became clear that the cameo had been left there for a reason. The killer was using it as a clue to his identity, which meant that, unless James unmasked him first, he would soon reveal himself, with potentially tragic consequences.

James was certain that he could uncover the meaning of the cameo. He just needed a little time. Perhaps the three flowers were some kind of symbol. Perhaps the same crest could be found in some sort of public place. It occurred to him that, as the cameo was most likely meant for Miss Fraser, she would be the best person to decipher its meaning. But the day had been difficult enough for her.

***

James stood outside of Miss Fraser's bedroom. She was aware he had intended to inspect the crime scene, and was undoubtedly expecting to hear something from him. Her connection with the victim gave her an especially strong emotional involvement in this incident; he felt a duty to give her what closure he could, without revealing the whole truth, as it would no doubt upset her.

He raised a hand to knock on the door, and instead found it gently creeping open under his fist. He could just make out Charlotte's voice, whispering something to Miss Fraser.

"I don't want to take the tonic!" Miss Fraser's voice rang through the room, loud and clear, and full of tears. It broke James's heart.

Charlotte whispered some more. Miss Fraser answered, "I don't want to stop crying. I should be crying. My friend is dead. And I was so horrible to her." Her voice broke over the last few words.

James took a few steps into the room, getting close enough to hear Charlotte's side of the conversation.

"...horrible. You only said what needed to be said. It's not your fault that Forrest chose that night to snap and kill her. It is a tragic accident of fate, nothing more." Charlotte looked up and saw James. "My brother is here. Do you want me to send him away?"

Miss Fraser shook her head. She took a big gulp of air, rubbed her face with both hands, trying desperately to regain some composure, at least in appearance.

"I'll give you a moment, then," Charlotte said. But rather than leave immediately, she grabbed James by the arm and dragged him back to the doorway. She then slapped his arm so hard, he would probably find a bruise there in the near future.

"Whatever you are planning to say to her, James, you better think twice about it. I won't allow you to upset her any further."

"I do not intend to. You must think I'm a complete idiot."

"Not a complete idiot, no."

And with one last glare, Charlotte left James alone with Miss Fraser.

He pulled a chair closer to the bed and sat in front of her. He took her hand, offering what comfort he could, and sat with her in silence, believing it better to let her speak first.

"Have you seen it, then?" she asked.

"Well, hmm, I saw the room. The, ahem, body, had already been removed."

Rose nodded. She was somewhat relieved by that answer. Had Mr. Grey seen Mary's body, she did not think she would have been able to resist asking for details, and she did not need that image in her head. The memory of their last conversation, the fact that she had shunned her friend in the last hours of her life, was terrible enough.

"Charlotte says that it was Mr. Forrest who did it. Do you agree?"

"The police believes it."

"I asked what you believed, sir."

Mr. Grey took a minute to answer. "There are inconsistencies in this theory."

James saw Miss Fraser raise her head. Her eyes were fixed on a point, somewhere on his jacket. He followed her gaze and saw the cameo hanging out of his pocket. He quickly stuffed it back in, well out of sight.

"Where did you get that?" asked Miss Fraser in a small voice.

"It's nothing to concern yourself with."

"It was there, wasn't it? It was with Mary?" Her voice grew louder as her anxiety rose.

"Miss Fraser..." James tried to think of a way to calm her down. Such agitation could not be good for her health.

"It was, it was," she repeated with great insistence, in the tone of a child who claims to have seen a monster; the obstinacy did nothing to detract from the terror.

"Miss Fraser," James tried once more, "this cameo could have found itself in that room in a great number of ways. It could have belonged to anyone."

"No. No, you don't understand!"

She scooted up the bed and grabbed a picture frame from her nightstand, thrusting it at him.

"Here. This is a picture of my parents. They were on their honeymoon in France. Look: my mother is wearing the same cameo."

And indeed she was, as far and James could tell. A small ivory disk depicting a crest bearing three flowers. "It had to have been him," Miss Fraser continued. "That man killed my mother, and he left the cameo there so I would know it was him, and what he did."

There were no consistent accounts of any missing items in the reports James could find of that night. Rather than to point that aloud, he said "This could be a copy, or one of many such designs."

"It couldn't be. This is the Fraser family crest. It was a wedding present from my father to my mother. It was one of a kind. And what does it matter if it was a copy? Do you not realize what this means? This is a message to me. He killed my mother and my father, and my friend, and now he's going to kill me."

"He won't. I won't let him." But James's words were lost on Miss Fraser. His hands on her shoulders failed to ground her in reality.

"You can't stop him! You don't even know who he is!"

He wished he did. He wished he had a name to give her, to give the police, so that this man could be apprehended and removed from her life. He knew he was close; he could feel it. He was missing something, just one little something, that one clue that would put everything in its place.

He wanted to plead for just a little more time, but looking at Miss Fraser, in such a state, was more than he could bear. He remembered the conversation he had with Albert and Charlotte. They were right. Miss Fraser's safety and her well-being were more important than his pride.

"I'll take you away, then," James said. "My father was working on obtaining a special license for us. I'm sure he'll have it by now. We'll elope, and take a long honeymoon on the continent. I'll turn my findings over to the police, or to another private detective if they won't listen to me. We'll stay away until that man is caught."

She stared at him as he spoke. Her breathing became less erratic; it appeared that what he said calmed her down ever so slightly. Suddenly, she threw herself in his arms. "I'm scared," she admitted in a trembling voice. He could feel her tears dampening his shirt. He pushed her back, fixed his eyes on hers.

"I promise you, I will do everything in my power to keep you safe."
After a moment, she nodded. She trusted him.

***

Even though they hardly knew Mary Jones, and liked her none at all, her murder proved to be too much excitement for the Londoners, and the party was soon broken up.

James used every excuse he could think of to delay his departure. He was expecting word from Will. They had agreed that the boy, or most likely the servant James sent with him, would send a telegram one fortnight after their separation, and the date fell two days after the murder of Mary Jones.

The day arrived, as it was bound to, and with it came the long awaited telegram.

Could not find either. [stop] Awaiting further instructions. [stop]

Could not find either?

James felt a shiver running down his spine as a thought entered his mind. Though he could not yet offer solid evidence, or even guess at a motive, he was beginning to suspect the identity of the killer of Mary Jones, Miss Fraser's tormentor.

He had many questions to answer, however, and should his suspicion be proven correct, he had very little time left to answer them. He sent his reply.

Returning to London. [stop] Will meet you at usual place. [stop]

Chapter 13

The Greys were the very last guests to leave the seaside mansion, and Rose with them. Mr. Grey rode ahead of the party as soon as the house was out of sight, and she was left with the quietly supportive presence of Lord and Lady Grey, and with her own thoughts.

Rose found herself in a very difficult position when she returned home; a position she had never found herself in before in her life. She was faced with the anger of both her guardians. Her aunt's feelings were still less than cordial, and her uncle, who had returned from his business trip the previous day, was inexplicably furious.

"Your things have been moved to the servants' quarters," declared Aunt Edwards coldly. "They will remain there until you are ready to move."

Rose was shocked. "Move, my aunt?"

"As your marriage with this Mr. Grey is no doubt imminent, I trust arrangements will be made for you to stay with those relatives of his. After those shenanigans by the seaside, you are no longer welcome in this house."

Shenanigans? Did her aunt mean Mary's murder? But why punish her for that? "But..."

153

"The only reason you have not already been thrown out is that Mr. Grey sent word asking to meet your uncle and me this evening. We can only hope that he is coming to declare his intentions, and that this matter can still be resolved with the appearance of propriety, if nothing else."

Rose turned to her uncle. She could scarcely believe the way he was glaring at her; never before had she seen this expression on his face. "Uncle..."

"The decision is final, Rose," declared her aunt, in a tone which left no room for doubt. "Robinson will show you to your room."

A shiver ran down Rose's spine. She would be alone with Robinson. Who could not describe the street urchins who used to deliver the notes. Who had been out when her uncle's carriage ran out of control. He said he went to the grocers, but he had been empty-handed. Who knew what he'd been up to the last few days? She was in no position to ask now. He had worked for her aunt and uncle for years, since before she was born. He had known her parents.

"Miss Fraser," said Robinson, very somberly, in his ever so proper tone. For the first time in her life, that voice chilled her to the bone. She tried to imagine that voice as a raspy whisper, calling out her first name.

She saw her maid Eliza standing just outside of the room. She ran to her and grabbed her arm. "Stay with me, Eliza."

"Miss?"

"Just do as I say, and do not leave me alone."

The maid was confused, but she knew better than to disobey a direct order from her mistress. Therefore, she remained at Rose's side as Robinson led the way to Rose's new and temporary quarters, and did not leave the room throughout the evening.

***

James was received rather coldly by Mr. and Mrs. Edwards. Though he bowed his head to them as he entered the sitting room, they did nothing to return the salute. Rather, Mr. Edwards abruptly announced that the discussion would be better suited for his office.

James found the office to be exactly what he had thought it would be. He took in the room in one gaze, overlooking the generic decor as he was looking for something specific. He found it at last, carefully placed on a small table, well in sight of everyone who cared to look.

"It was good of you to receive me on such short notice," began James.

"As if we had a choice, in the wake of your disgraceful behavior."

James was not sure what to make of Mrs. Edwards's comment. "I beg your pardon?"

"And well you should. It has been reported to us by very reliable sources that you and our niece have become quite intimate during your seaside escapade. Constantly seeking each other's company, taking long, unchaperoned walks. What do you have to say for yourself?"

James remembered a previous conversation with Miss Fraser. She had warned him then of the expectations that would arise, should they spend much time in each other's exclusive company, and how those expectations could complicate the investigation. He saw then as he did now the wisdom of her words, and he regretted not paying better attention to them.

He had no problem dealing with the consequences of his lapse of judgment. He would be expected to marry Miss Fraser, and it was indeed not only his intention, but also one of his greatest desires, to do so. He only wished he had a little more time. He had promised Miss Fraser that he would marry her immediately, elope if he needed to, to keep her safe. But that was before he read Will's telegram, before he began to suspect the identity of her tormentor.

If he could prove his new theory, he would be able to get the fiend arrested, and make her truly safe. The answer was right in front of him, as clear as day. He only needed some concrete evidence, something to bring to the police.

"Mrs. Edwards, Mr. Edwards. I'm afraid that I had not realized how improper my actions would appear. I was carried away by my feelings for your niece. However, let me assure you, most emphatically, that my intentions are honorable. With your blessing, sir, madam, I do declare that it would be my great privilege to make Miss Fraser my bride."

"No."

Mr. Edwards's answer shocked his wife, who could do no more than stare at him. James was also surprised, and yet he found that one-word answer so very revealing. It was, at least, the beginning of an answer to many other questions he could not ask aloud.

"Why should I consent to this? You think that you're so important? That you can just come here and pretend to ask, while really you come to take? As good as thievery, this blessing nonsense."

Mrs. Edwards had recovered enough to whisper her husband's name.

"I understand your hesitation, Mr. Edwards," James said calmly as he made his way across the room. "How I must appear to you! A young man, with little more than my father's name and a, shall we say, peculiar employment. Whereas you, you are a proper businessman. And even more, a war hero."

James was now in front of the small table which held Mr. Edwards's various medals.

"I see you were wounded in the Pacific in fifty-five."

"That does not concern you!" Mr. Edwards snatched the medal James had casually picked up and slammed it back against the table.

"Mr. Grey." Mrs. Edwards had recovered her wits, and was determined to act, for the sake of their reputation. "It is very wise of you to recognize how protective my husband and I are of Rose. We see her quite as our own. I am afraid everyone here is too emotional to deal with this matter rationally. Let us sleep on it, and tomorrow we may discuss with clearer minds."

She rang the bell before either man could protest. Robinson appeared immediately. "Until tomorrow, Mr. Grey."

James had no choice. He bowed to his hosts and, escorted by Robinson, made his way to his carriage.

Once the Edwards's residence was no longer in sight, James turned to Will, who had been concealed in the carriage all afternoon. "Did you see him?" he asked the boy.

"Yeah." The answer was muffled, as Will was biting his thumbnail.

"And you're sure it was the same man?"

"Yeah!" From his tone, it was clear Will expected the answer to be obvious. He suddenly removed his hand from his mouth. "Do you think he saw me?"

"He didn't mention it. He probably forgot all about you, if it makes you feel better."

Will's bitter laugh indicated that his lack of memorability did not, in fact, make him feel any better. James ignored the boy's nerves and ordered his driver to get to the closest police station.

"Wait, what? I'm not going there!"

"Well then, you better get out of this carriage, because I am." James was determined, and there was no room for discussion. "Something terrible is about to happen, tonight in all probability. And I will do everything in my power to prevent it."

***

In the dark, all alone, Rose waited.

The evening had been simply terrible. Eliza remained in her room, as she had been ordered to do, and the two of them listened in on the worst argument she had ever witnessed between her aunt and uncle.

"You have completely lost your mind, George! Or are you determined to ruin us all?"

"I will not tolerate your hysteria tonight, Louisa."

"Hysteria!! My concern for our social standing, for our chances of advancing in society..."

"You are the only one who cares about such things! We will never see those people again, what they think of us is irrelevant!"

"I cannot understand you. After everything that happened, after the damage to our reputation, how can you not insist that he marry her as soon as possible?"

"My decision is made, and the subject is closed."

"You listen to me, you foolish man. I have worked too long and too hard for this moment, and I will not..."

Aunt Edwards interrupted herself with a cry of pain as the sound of a slap resounded. Rose could hardly believe what she heard. Her uncle behaved like a man possessed.

"Whew," breathed Eliza. "I've only seen them go at it that bad once before, when the missus sent you crying to the attic."

Eliza's words were not encouraging.

"I wonder why Mr. Edwards doesn't want you to marry Mr. Grey," the maid continued.

"Don't be ridiculous, Eliza. There is no reason for him to object to the marriage. Certainly the argument is about something else." After a few moments of consideration, Rose found what. "It must be the manner of the wedding he objects to. The Baron of Rotherfield is working to obtain a special license for us, to get married sooner."

"You and Mr. Grey are eloping, miss?"

"In a manner of speaking. That must be what my uncle objects to. He must wish for a proper wedding, while my aunt has somehow convinced herself that the wedding must occur as soon as possible. That must be what the argument is about."

"Of course, miss."

No matter what the cause had been, the argument, and the tension between herself and her aunt and uncle, kept Rose in her room, and Eliza with her. The maid had been so good, remaining at her mistress's side through the evening, without dinner, that when the time came to turn in for the night, Rose did not have the heart to detain her further.

And so she lay, in the dark, listening to the house. Every sound seemed suspicious, keeping her awake and alert. She told herself that she only had one such night to endure. Mr. Grey would come back in the morning and take her to his sister-in-law's house.

She heard footsteps in the corridor; too slow, too quiet, too deliberate to be anything but menacing. Her bedroom door opened, much in the same way: slowly, quietly, deliberately, menacingly.

She was out of time.

She closed her eyes, not wanting to see death come for her, and reopened them when a hand abruptly fell against her mouth. The first thing she noticed was the knife. The second was the face of the man holding it, the face of a man she never would have believed could behave in this manner.

"Get up!" ordered Uncle Edwards.

Chapter 11

The circulation on the streets was a nightmare, as it usually was when one was in a hurry. James did his best not to panic, and used the time to think about how to best present his appeal.

He had not been certain how he would convince the police to listen to him; he did not have as many convincing elements as he would have hoped for. He had friends in almost every station of London, he made a point of it, but it might be a lot to ask in the name of friendship. He would have to do a lot of fast talking.

James had not realized, had never even considered the possibility that he would not get the chance to talk at all. The scene that played before his eye as he reached the police station was so far beyond his imagination that he could only stare in shock.

The men were assembled on the sidewalk, too many of them to imagine that there could be anyone left inside. A few of them were carrying signs. The messages varied, but one word was repeated in several instances: strike.

"What is this madness?" asked James as he exited the carriage.

Many men noticed him, and one sergeant - a man named Brown, if he recalled correctly - approached him. He was no friend of James, unfortunately. Sergeant Brown had never made a secret of his belief that bored, pampered, rich children such as James had no business interfering with law enforcement. James's moderate success in his endeavors did not influence his opinion the smallest bit.

"Well well, if it isn't Lord Grey himself, gracing us with his presence. How d'you do, milord?"

"This farce is of very poor taste, Sergeant."

"What farce?"

"This strike business. You cannot be serious."

"Oh, but we are. We're damn serious. We've got three divisions in on the strike, we've got an MP speaking for us at Parliament and writing to the papers. Even Bow Street is in. The Commissioner, and the Home Secretary, and all of them, they'll realize that we won't be worked to the bone for pennies and shillings anymore. We'll get what we're owed."

"This is about money?" James could not believe what he had heard. "Do you not realize what you're doing? You are forsaking your sworn duty, inviting anarchy and chaos. And all for money?!"

"It's easy enough for you to take that tone, sir. You spend more in a week than most of us make in a year, and we have families to feed."

"It will never work. What will happen is that you will all be suspended, and more than likely dismissed altogether. Some of you might be allowed to return to work, if you are lucky. There are plenty of men out there who would be grateful for your pennies and shillings."

Brown turned back toward the others. "March on, men! To the park!"

A frustrated and befuddled James watched the policemen march away. He considered going to a different station, but feared he would get the same result over and over again. If the strike was as important as Brown had declared it to be, if it continued to spread...

James had to face the facts: he was on his own.

***

It was the second time Rose found herself in this attic, trying to regain control of her emotions. This time, however, she was not alone.

She watched as her uncle paced in front of her. He was even more agitated than she was. She did not fully comprehend what was going on, or why. However, she knew that she had to remain calm. Her survival depended upon it.

"You will not marry him," Uncle Edwards finally said. "I forbid it."

Rose struggled with the urge to ask why. She instinctively knew that it would be a dangerous question to ask at this moment. "As you wish, uncle."

"I mean it, Rose."

"I know. You must believe me, uncle, I would never take such a step without your approval."

"You did it once before!"

Uncle Edwards's sudden outburst made Rose jump back in fear.

"What do you mean?"

He did not answer her right away, but instead took a few shaking breaths. "I mean... when you agreed to come to this godforsaken town. When you agreed, against my express wishes, to sell yourself to the highest bidder on the marriage mart."

"I did not realize how much you disliked the idea."

"I told you how much I disliked it. I told you again and again, but you did not listen!"

"The notes." Rose had figured out as much, but somehow, she had not believed until the words slipped out of her mouth. "I... I'm sorry, uncle," she said, trying to steady her voice. "I should have realized."

Uncle Edwards resumed his pacing. Rose, unsure what to say, remained silent.

"This is all her fault," he finally said. "None of this would have happened if not for her."

Rose was afraid to ask, and yet she felt she had to. "Whose fault, uncle?"

"Louisa." Rose shuddered as he spit out her aunt's Christian name.

"It was all on her, right from the beginning. I never should have married her. I didn't even want to. Father said it was good business, a way to get the buildings he wanted at a bargain. Bargain for him, maybe. He didn't understand. No one understood. Louisa least of all. She tried to keep us apart from the beginning. Acted as though she had the right to barrel in and ruin our lives. Called herself the lady of the house, treated Florence like an unwanted guest."

Florence? Her mother?

"We were twins!" continued Uncle Edwards. "We were of the same flesh and blood, united from the womb. We belonged together!

"But Louisa didn't care about that. Oh no. And Father and Mother were just as bad. Whenever I came to visit Florence, or when I invited her to stay with us, Louisa would complain to them, and they would reprimand me, tell me I should be taking better care of my wife. The nerve! And, when that didn't work, they sent me to war. Packed me on that bloody ship, said it was my duty. Ha! Some duty. It was all a trap. I came back over a year later to find they married her off.

"They would not tell me to whom, or where she went. Said it was for the best. Well, I took care of them. They interfered with my life one time too many. I should have taken care of Louisa then, too, but I had to find Florence. It took me years; first to even discover where she went, and then... Do you have any idea how big this city is? But I did it. Eventually, I did find her. But when I did... she said that she couldn't leave you. Of course, I told her to bring you along. A child should not be separated from her mother, and I had every intention of providing for both of you. But then she said that she couldn't leave him. They had turned her against me."

"Oh, uncle." Through the horror that had washed over her, Rose found a shred of pity for him. "You loved her." But that shred was so thin, so quickly run through. "And yet, that night..."

"Rose... you have to understand, I didn't mean to. I never meant to harm her. Please believe me."

"I do believe you, uncle. I understand. When she did not leave, it made you angry."

"How could she do this to me? How could she? But even then, I would not have harmed her. Only, he came into the room. He had stolen her from me. It was his fault. And I found myself standing over him, with my knife. But then, Florence was screaming, and she would not stop, and the servants were coming, and I panicked. I didn't even realize what I was doing until it was over. Do you see, Rose? I felt terrible, afterward. I kept thinking about Florence, what I had done to her. And I thought about you. A little baby, innocent. I returned to the house the next day, and I took the necessary steps to become your guardian. Louisa was unhappy, but it was already done. I was determined to take care of you. You would not suffer your mother's fate, not as long as I watched over you."

Though she tried to conceal it, Rose felt nauseous, as her uncle justified his crimes. She would not have been surprised to learn that her mother had been afraid of him, that her marriage had been a means of escaping an overly possessive brother.

There was no doubt in Rose's mind that Uncle Edwards was responsible for what had happened to Mary. But she did not understand; how would killing her friend ensure that she would remain unmarried? Was there even an explanation behind this act, or had her uncle somehow completely descended into madness?

168

She might have feared the answer. She might have feared the anger that the mere question could provoke. But, for some strange reason, Rose was most of all afraid of her uncle's silence.

So, in a timid voice, she asked, "Uncle, what happened to Mary?"

"I could ask you the same, Rose," answered Uncle Edwards. "What happened to Mary? You two were friends, and all of a sudden, you refuse to associate with her? Why is that, Rose? Because your aunt told you to, wasn't it? Because that boy and his family pressured you? They didn't like her anti-marriage stance, they felt threatened by it, and so they forced you to stop seeing her, is that it?"

"And now she's dead," Rose said softly.

"Well, there was no point in keeping her alive, if you would not listen to her."

"It's my fault." The words twirled around in her head so busily that Rose barely heard herself say them out loud. She jumped when her uncle put a hand on her shoulder.

"I'm sorry I had to go to this extreme, Rose, but do you understand, now, that it was necessary?"

She understood no such thing, and, in fact, she was convinced of the opposite. Yet, she nodded.

"Good. Now, this is what will happen. I'll go take care of your aunt. Tomorrow, after the police are gone and all the other nonsense is dealt with, we will leave this cursed town and never return. We will go back home. I'll go back to my business, you can run the house, play the piano all day long, never have to worry about getting married. Doesn't that sound nice?"

It might have, three months ago. Now it sounded horrible. Still, Rose nodded again.

"Excellent. Wait here."

Uncle Edwards began to walk toward the attic door. He was about to go kill Aunt Edwards: Rose knew it, as surely as she knew her own name. She had to find a way to stop him, or live with the death of her aunt on her conscience.

But how?

"Uncle," she called out, trying to hide her desperation. "May we not leave now? Just... leave Aunt Edwards behind. You can get a divorce, I'm sure you can think of some reason. There's no need to... harm her, is there?"

Uncle Edwards sighed. "You are a sensitive soul, Rose; I would not expect you to understand. She's been meddling with my life for far too long."

On those words, Uncle Edwards left the room. Rose could only stare as the lock loudly clicked into place.

She had to do something. She had to get help, somehow, and soon, or her aunt would die. But there was no way to get help. She was locked in the room. She could try to scream, but her uncle was sure to hear, and then...

Rose remembered her uncle's words, about the night he killed her parents: "Florence was screaming, and she would not stop..."

No, she could not scream. She had no way of getting help. Her aunt was going to die, and it would be her fault. Just like it was her fault Mary had died.

Unless...

Once the idea hit her, she ran with it without thinking, and without pause; there was no time to lose. She gathered what she needed: an old and tattered gown, an iron cooking pot, the square of flint she had seen earlier. She stuffed the gown into the pot, carried it all to the window, and began to strike the pot with the flint.

Sparks flew but did not catch. She struck the pot again, and again, frantically. Until, finally, smoke started to rise from the pot, weakly at first, but then stronger and thicker. Rose grabbed a rag and fanned the smoke away from her and out the window. She could already hear people on the street calling for firemen. The relief those voices gave her was too great for words. The firemen would come, they would stop her uncle, they would save her aunt. Everything would be all right.

As the thought crossed her mind, a sudden burst of flames seemed to jump out of the pot. It caught onto the windowsill and started quickly spreading. Rose had no way out.

Chapter 15

The search might seem fruitless, even desperate, but James could not, would not, allow himself to give up. Someone, somewhere, would listen to him. After the unsuccessful meeting with Sergeant Brown, he went to two other stations, where he met similar opposition and obtained the same result.

It occurred to him then that he might have better luck in the other direction. The strike madness most likely had a flow, which he must have been following, and he might find more reasonable minded men by going against the current, so to speak.

This was how he found himself going past the Edwards's household once more. As the carriage approached the house, something caught his attention, which took his mind away from the strike, away from the villain, away from everything except this immediate matter.

He detected smoke escaping from the attic window.

He ordered his carriage to a halt and jumped out, rushing to the house. He had to get Miss Fraser out.

As made his way inside the house, he considered asking for help from a domestic, but reasoned that he would waste precious time trying to explain his presence in the house, and that it would be more expedient to simply search the house himself. He assumed that, at this hour, Miss Fraser would be in her bedchambers, and that those would not be located on the first floor. Therefore, with the smell of the smoke teasing his nostrils and urging him forward, he started to climb.

He had climbed the first flight of stairs when he came face to face with George Edwards, making his own way down the same stairs, holding a knife.

"You!" Mr. Edwards growled the word, before he threw himself at James, charging like a wild animal. James barely had time to evade him. And even at that, he did not quite succeed, as the two men still tripped over each other's feet.

James regained his balance. Mr. Edwards did not. He fell about half-way down the stairs, and did not get back up again. James stared at the corpse, breathing heavily, feeling very confused.

Before he had any time to truly comprehend what had just happened, the smell of the smoke coming from somewhere above his head grew even stronger. He had to find Miss Fraser right now.

As the thought formed in his mind, he heard a young woman's voice crying out from above. It was Miss Fraser. He ran up to the attic.

***

It was a living nightmare. Though the flames could not find purchase on the brick walls, they quickly made their way across the floor and the ceiling. The oppressive heat weighed on Rose, making her feel lethargic. Thick black smoke filled the room, and it was becoming impossible to breathe.

Rose was crouched beside the door, putting as much distance between herself and the flames as she could. The air was easier to breathe, closer to the ground, but not by much. There was nothing she could do but hope for a miracle.

That miracle came: someone was forcefully knocking at the door. "Miss Fraser!"

Was that Mr. Grey?

Did it matter?

"Help! Help! I can't get out! The door is locked!"

The knocks moved to the wall next to the door. "Move here. To this side of the door. I'll open it, just get out of the way."

Rose dragged herself across the floor until she was clear of the door. She then knocked on the wall. "All right, I did it." Rose barely managed to speak this once sentence, before she was overcome with coughing.

After what felt like an eternity of waiting, the door finally opened, and Mr. Grey was standing over her.

He grabbed her and lifted her to her feet, then dragged her out of the room. "Can you run?" he asked. Rose shook her head; her leg was still throbbing painfully, and her lungs burned from the smoke. He picked her up without another word and carried her downstairs.

Though the flight down the stairs and out of the house was very quick, it would have been impossible for Rose not to notice her uncle's body blocking the way out. Mr. Grey struggled to avoid the body and keep his grip on her, but he succeeded, and soon, they were out.

Once they were safe, Mr. Grey placed her back on her feet. "Mr. Grey," Rose started hesitantly, gasping for breath, "how... that was... my uncle, and... you're here... what..."

"I can explain, I promise," he interrupted. "But not now. I'm really not supposed to be here. I'll come back tomorrow morning, and on my word, I'll explain everything then."

The promise satisfied Rose, who nodded in agreement. Mr. Grey returned the nod, staring at her in a daze. He suddenly wrapped his arms around her, holding her tightly.   She took comfort in his embrace, finally able to believe, for the first time in weeks, that all would be well.

He eventually let go of her. "You should go back to your aunt. I'll see you in the morning." And on these words, he turned and left. Rose walked backwards slowly, keeping her eyes on him for as long as he was in sight.

It was only when she could no longer distinguish his figure in the darkness that she turned and walked to the street, where her aunt was arguing with a fireman about breaking furniture and dragging dirt all around the house.

Chapter 16

The next morning, James returned to the Edwards's household, as he had promised he would. The sitting room where he was brought was much as it had been; thankfully, the firemen had reached the house quickly, and the fire had not spread much to the lower levels.

There was, however, a great deal of change in the inhabitants of the house. He found Mrs. Edwards waiting for him; at the very least, he assumed it was Mrs. Edwards. She was dressed in full mourning clothes, including a very thick, almost opaque black veil which completely dissimulated her features, but who else could it be?

"Mr. Grey," the voice behind the veil said, and it became obvious that it was, indeed, Mrs. Edwards. "I am afraid that the situation has changed since we last spoke. You see, my husband was found dead last night. I can only assume that, had you known, you would not have come today. You must already be aware that it would be improper to plan for a wedding while we are in mourning. A complete withdrawal from society is expected of both of us, for a year at the very least, as you know. Perhaps in the future..."

Mrs. Edwards was interrupted by the arrival of Miss Fraser. Something about the new arrival shocked the newly-widowed woman, if the gasp of horror escaping from behind the veil was to be believed.

"Rose! How dare you show yourself dressed in this indecent manner? Today, of all days! You will go back to your room and change this instant."

Miss Fraser looked down, staring at her dark burgundy dress for a few, very tense, moments, before raising her head once more. "I must confess that I do not understand you, my aunt. My dress seems perfectly decent to me. On the other hand, the act of wearing black to mark the death of the man who murdered my parents, that seems indecent."

Silence fell once more on the sitting room, weighing heavily. Miss Fraser seemed to detect something in the silence, in her aunt's manner, that escaped James's attention. "You knew," she said. "You knew what he did! How could you stay with him?"

"A wife's duty is to remain by her husband's side. Besides, she only got what she deserved."

"How can you say that?"

"She was always there, like a stray cat, letting herself be rubbed and begging for scraps. Running off with the first man who would take her, having you less than a year later."

"And what did my father do, to deserve death?"

"He was a rogue; he had the most awful reputation. His elopement with your mother was the last in a long string of scandals. No one mourned him."

"What about my grand-parents? What about you? Uncle Edwards killed them, and he was planning to kill you as well. He said so himself."

"I do not believe that. Your grandfather died in a hunting accident, and your grandmother died in her sleep."

"He confessed to me, my aunt."

"I do not believe you! And we have discussed this nonsense for long enough. Go up and change. We are leaving soon."

"No."

Miss Fraser's answer shocked the words out of Mrs. Edwards.

"I will not change, and you may leave, but I will not. I will avoid paying social calls, and going out in the evening. I will dress somberly, though not in black. I will do these things, for three months, which is a more than acceptable mourning period for so distant a relative as an uncle. I will do these things out of respect for you, who took me in when you could have turned me away. But I will not return to the North with you, and I will not delay my wedding with Mr. Grey for more than two years. Assuming, of course, that he still wishes to marry me."

James could do little more than nod. Miss Fraser's bold declaration and her firm stance humbled him into silence. Mrs. Edwards did not seem to react, at first. But then she slowly rose and rang the bell.

"Robinson," she told the butler when he appeared, "you will dispose of the girl's possessions. Let her take them where she please, it is none of our concerns anymore."

Robinson nodded as his mistress left the room.

Once Mrs. Edwards was well out of sight, the butler turned to Miss Fraser. "I'll see to your belongings, Miss."

"Do you think it would be possible for me to take Eliza? I would very much like to keep her in my service, and I can't imagine my aunt would have much use for her."

"I'll arrange it." Robinson bowed to Miss Fraser and made to leave the room. He turned to face her at the last moment. "I'm sorry it came to this, Miss Rose."

"Thank you, Robinson."

Robinson left then, and James found himself alone with Miss Fraser.

"Now I feel bad that I suspected him," she said. "It was my uncle, did you know that? He sent the letters and he killed Mary, and my parents."

"I know. I had realized as much last night."

"How? And how could you be sure it wasn't Robinson?"

"I eliminated Robinson as a suspect fairly early in the investigation. I talked to someone your uncle had tried to hire to deliver the notes to you, and he described a tall man, which Robinson is not. Bernadette gave the same description of the Mr. Smith who paid her for the chance to talk to you alone. As for how I knew it was your uncle...

"While we were all at the seaside, I sent someone to look for an origami school up in your hometown, where the man who sent you these letters might have studied, and to talk to your uncle if he could manage it. He found neither the school nor your uncle. Your uncle had lied about his destination, which made him look suspicious. The deaths of your grandparents, in this new context, seemed awfully convenient. The carriage incident could have been staged; he did not lose control, but rather drove recklessly on purpose. When I saw that he had been injured in the Pacific, and that he spent a few months in a Japanese hospital, it was the missing piece of the puzzle.

"I wasn't sure about the motive, although I now suspect that it was related to your aunt's declarations, this morning, concerning your mother. I'm afraid I handled the matter rather poorly. That this man would set the attic on fire and lock you in, because I..."

"Oh, he didn't," interrupted Miss Fraser. "That is, he did lock me in the attic, but he didn't set in on fire. That was me."

James stared at Miss Fraser, unblinking, in silence. "I beg your pardon?" he finally said.

"Well, I didn't mean to, really. I only meant to set an old dress on fire, and it was in a big cooking pot, and I thought that it would make smoke, and that someone would see and call the firemen. My uncle had said that he was going to kill my aunt, and he locked me in the attic. I was afraid that if I screamed, he would get angry with me and kill me. I didn't realize that the fire would jump out of the pot like that. Why are you laughing at me?"

James tried to regain his composure, with little success. "I'm sorry. You do realize, though, that there's a reason we put fire screens in front of fireplaces? Fire tends to do that, jump in any direction."

"Well I didn't know." Miss Fraser mumbled, lowering her face towards the floor. Her pitiful expression stopped James's laughter cold.

"I truly am sorry. I should not be laughing. I just... I don't like thinking about what could have happened to you. I'm glad you were not hurt."

"Thanks to you," Miss Fraser whispered. For a moment, neither said anything.

"I suppose it's time to go," James finally said. "Would you allow me to escort you to my brother's house?"

"Yes, thank you." Miss Fraser hesitated, before she continued. "Are you sure you don't mind?"
"Escorting you? Of course not, or I would not have offered."

"No, not that. Waiting three months, for the wedding. It might seem strange to you, considering what he has done, but he is... I mean, he was my uncle, and he just died. It doesn't feel right."

James held both of Miss Fraser's hands in his, and stared into her eyes. "I would have waited two years for you. I would wait until the end of time for you. Three months is nothing. Take the time you need. I want our wedding day to be perfect."

She smiled brightly at him, and it was as though she was reading his mind, for she voiced his thoughts as soon as he had formed them: "I can't imagine it will be any other way."

They walked out of the house arm in arm.

Acknowledgements

Thank you to my parents. Thank you for life, I enjoy that. Thank you also for my education, for the overflowing bookshelves of my childhood, and for never denying me a book.

In the same spirit, thank you to my Grandmother, Céline, who was a great reader herself and could always be relied upon to give a book on a special occasion. To the teachers who would let me read my novels in class - once I had finished the assignments, of course - and to those who went a step further and recommended books to me.

One last thank you in this line of thoughts, thank you to the authors I have read, those I am reading, and those I will read in the future. Writers are readers. First, last and always.

Thank you to the friendly doctors and the camp counsellors who would listen to me talk about my stories, and offer what help and encouragement they could. You were the first ones who made me feel that I had something special, something to help define me.

Thank you to Manon, to Jessica, to Marie-Claude, to Diane, to Odette, to Murielle. The story of The Admirer had been in my head for almost a decade by the time we met.

It might have stayed there a decade more if not for you, my first audience, who expected me to read you a scene every other week. I owe the first draft to you.

Thank you to the team at Renaissance Press, who helped me take that first draft, polish it, and make the novel as it now exists.

A special thank you to Caroline. You were part of that first audience, and you are the creator of the beautiful cover, but you are more than that. When we met, I had stopped going to camp, and the friendly doctors had retired. I had forgotten that I had something special, and you reminded me. You told me that I was good, that I was publishable, and you made me believe it. Thank you, for everything.

(That would have been an awesome last acknowledgement, but there is one group of important people I don't want to forget; thank you to the friends and family who have given me the most positive, the most heartwarming encouragement I have ever heard: "When is your book coming out it French? I want to read it!" Patience, grasshoppers.)

About the Author

Aurelia Osborne is the pen name of a Canadian author, born and raised in the National Capital Region. She studied Literature, Art History, translation, and creative writing. She hates talking about herself, especially in the third person. The Admirer is her first novel.